DESERTS

INFORMATION AND HANDS-ON ACTIVITIES

Robin Bernard

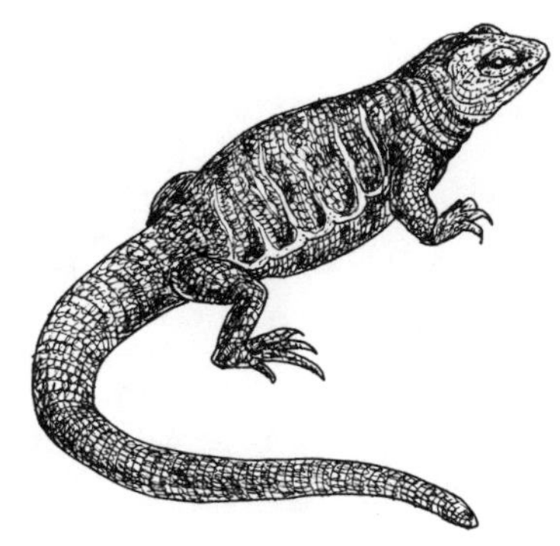

NEW YORK • TORONTO • LONDON • AUCKLAND • SYDNEY

DEDICATION

As always, in all ways, for Jerry. And for our daughters Pamela, Stephanie, and Adrienne.

●

ACKNOWLEDGMENTS

Endless thanks to Liza Charlesworth who makes these projects such a pleasure;
to Terry Cooper for encouraging the explorations;
and to Mkwebe Melubo for leading me into the Kaisut desert.

Cover design by Frank Maiocco
Interior design by Solutions by Design, Inc.
Interior illustrations by Robin Bernard
Photo research by Daniella Jo Nilva

Cover Photography: Sonoran Desert—© Jeffrey Muir Hamilton/Liaison International; Sand Dunes and Hedgehog Cactus—© Stan Osolinski/Dembinsky Photo Assoc.; Frilled Lizard—© Karl H. Switak/Photo Researchers, Inc.

ISBN 0-590-49801-0

TABLE OF CONTENTS

SAND, SCORPIONS, AND SNOW

Most of us imagine deserts as oceans of sand—vast, barren, and baking beneath a blazing sun. But that image is only part of the desert story. Most of the world's deserts do have high daytime temperatures. The Mohave and the Sahara are good examples. But some deserts, such as the Gobi and our own Great Basin, are in fact *cold* deserts. For part of the year these cold deserts have daytime temperatures below freezing, and much of their meager moisture comes from snow! And that's only one surprise—deserts are full of them. Their barren appearance is misleading, for an amazing variety of wildlife and plants have evolved adaptations enabling them to survive the harsh environment. Even more surprising is the number of humans who live in arid areas: one out of every seven people on Earth!

This book is designed to introduce your students to a variety of fascinating desert ecosystems through a series of fun-filled learning activities—including games, graphs, experiments, and crafts. Some of the words used in the student material may be new to the children. Look for definitions in the text and also in the Glossary (page 55).

DEFINING DESERTS

The major deserts are spread across five continents. Some are sandy, while others have surfaces of rocks, pebbles, cracked mud, or salt. But all deserts have two characteristics that define them:

- less than 10 inches of rainfall a year, and
- a very high evaporation rate.

Desert rain doesn't fall a little at a time, nor is it predictable. Most deserts don't have a rainy season. When rain does arrive, it's often in brief torrential bursts that run off the hard-packed surface and evaporate before soaking into the soil. Most hot deserts lie in high atmospheric pressure zones, which have little or no cloud cover. This causes some of the most extreme temperature swings on Earth—as much as 75°F in 12 hours! Daytime temperatures soar rapidly in the sun's heat, and at night, with no cloud cover to hold in the heat, temperatures plunge.

DIFFERENT KINDS OF DESERTS

Deserts are usually formed by a combination of conditions, but there are four basic kinds.

INLAND DESERTS: Winds that sweep in from the ocean are full of moisture. As these wet winds move over land they rise, cool, and release the moisture as rain. But some places are simply too far from a coast to reap the benefits of those moisture laden winds. By the time they've swept across hundreds and hundreds of miles and reach the middle of a large land mass, nearly all the moisture has already fallen. An example of an inland desert is the Gobi Desert in Mongolia.

HIGH-PRESSURE DESERTS: Air circulates over the Earth in set patterns which cause zones of permanent high and low atmospheric pressure. In low pressure zones—like those near the equator—warm, humid air rises, forms clouds, and rains. This is why the tropics are so wet. In contrast, most deserts aren't located under these low pressure zones. Instead, they are under the nearly cloudless skies of high pressure zones north and south of the equator, often near the tropic of Cancer and tropic of Capricorn. When the rain-spent tropical air circulates and descends from the equatorial regions to these high pressure zones, it warms. This dry, warmed air evaporates what little moisture is present in the desert's atmosphere before it gets a chance to fall as rain. So no rain is brought in, nor is it allowed to fall. Examples of high pressure deserts on the African continent are the Sahara, under the northern high-pressure band, and the Kalahari, under the southern band.

That's a Fact
The Gobi Desert can have winter temperatures as low as -40°F.

RAIN-SHADOW DESERTS: A mountain range acts as a rain barrier. As air masses move from ocean to land, they're forced upwards as they strike a mountain range. As the masses rise, moisture condenses into clouds and falls as rain. By the time the winds cross over to the far side of the mountain peaks, the rain is depleted, and a rain-shadow desert results on the other side. The Patagonian Desert in South America is an example of one, as is the Great Basin Desert in the United States.

Here's how it works:

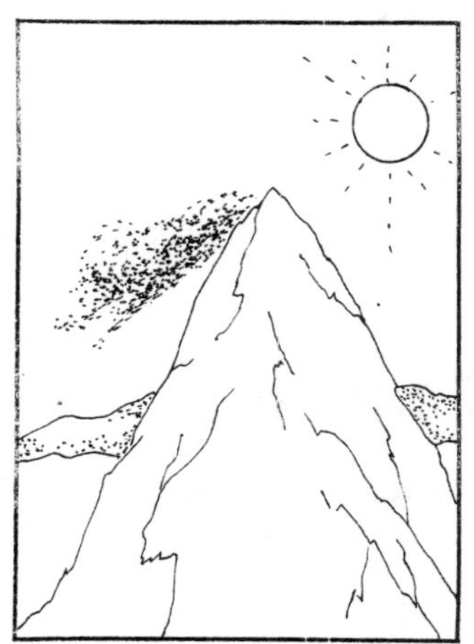

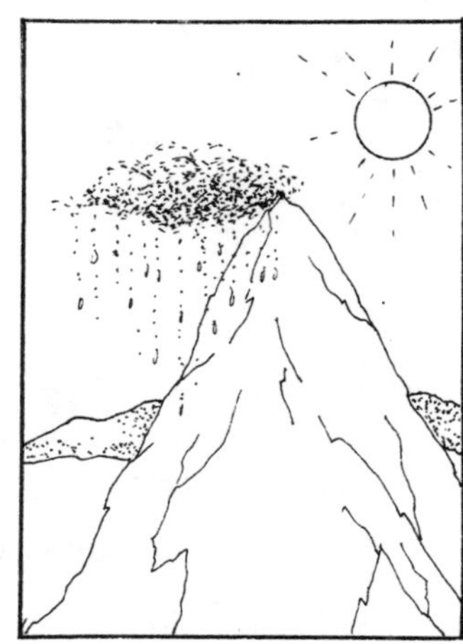

FOG DESERTS: Icy ocean currents move from the poles toward the tropics along the western coasts of continents. But cold wind over cold water carries very little moisture, so deserts often form along these coasts. And while rain is almost nonexistent, these deserts are cool and usually blanketed by fog caused by cold ocean currents colliding with hot winds blowing

off the land. The Atacama Desert in Chile, and the Namib Desert in southern Africa—both fog deserts—are two of the driest places on Earth! (The Atacama gets an average annual rainfall of less than $\frac{1}{25}$th of an inch!)

STUDENT ACTIVITIES

Spadefoot Toad KWL Chart

Here's a way for younger students to keep track of what they know about deserts, what they'd like to find out, and to share what they've learned. They can write questions and facts on toads.

1. Make copies of the spadefoot toad on page 8. Have the children color some yellow, some pale green, and some pink.

2. Divide a bulletin board into three parts, with the third section twice the size of the first two. Label the first: What We Know About Deserts; label the second: What We Want to Find Out About Deserts; and label the third: What We've Learned About Deserts.

3. Ask the children to brainstorm facts they already know, such as "Deserts are very dry," or "Roadrunners are desert birds." Record each fact on a yellow spadefoot toad and attach to the first section. Then have students talk about what they'd like to find out, such as "Are there any deserts where it's cold?" or "How long can a camel go without drinking?" Ask them to write their questions on pink toads, which can be taped to the second bulletin board section. As their questions are answered over the course of the unit, the new facts can be written on green toads and taped to the third section.

NOTE: *Older students may want to form cooperative groups and simply list the KWL facts and questions directly on oaktag.*

EXTENSION ACTIVITY: Leftover unanswered questions from the What We Want to Find Out About Deserts section could be assigned as group library research projects.

That's a Fact
In 1973, the Atacama Desert had torrential rains, but until that time, it hadn't rained for 400 years!

Where Are the Deserts?

1. Display the World Deserts poster where the students can see it. As you point out desert areas, explain how and where the four basic kinds of desert form. Challenge children to find examples of each. Point out the equator and the tropics of Cancer and Capricorn. Show them how to find the name of each continent, desert, and its size. Ask a student to define the word *coast* and to indicate some coastlines on the poster. Review North-East-South-West.

2. Make photocopies of page 9. Ask children to answer the questions using the poster as a reference.

***EXTENSION ACTIVITY*:** Using information from the poster, students can compare the size of specific deserts to one another, to countries, and to continents.

The King of the Deserts

Make copies of page 10 and distribute. Then challenge students to use the map to answer the questions. Explain that the enlarged map of the desert relates to the shaded area of the continent shown in the inset.

***EXTENSION ACTIVITY*:** Demonstrate the scale of the Sahara using your classroom. If your classroom were Africa, how much of it would be the Sahara Desert? Mark off this area with masking tape or yarn.

That's a Fact
The Sahara Desert is about a third of the African continent.

Rain, Rain, Come Again

1. Make photocopies of pages 11 and 12 to distribute.
2. Discuss the definition of *annual rainfall* with students. Ask: Does it all fall at once? The average rainfall of eight desert cities is listed on the student page.
3. Ask children to convert this information into bar graphs to compare rainfall and answer the questions. Students can use different colored pencils or crayons for each city.

***EXTENSION ACTIVITY*:** Ask students to guess what the annual rainfall is in their own town or city. (You can write examples from the Annual Rainfall of Cities Around the World sidebar on the board as hints.) Pass around a sheet of paper on which they each write their names and guesstimates. Then challenge children to find the actual local annual rainfall. The student who guesses closest can be accorded a rain dance performed by his or her classmates. The local annual rainfall can be graphed alongside the desert cities for comparison.

Annual Rainfall of Cities Around the World (inches)

Anchorage	14.6
Chicago	33.9
Denver	15.3
El Paso	7.8
Hong Kong	85.2
London	23.3
Miami	58.8
Moscow	24.6
Nairobi	37.8
New Orleans	59.7
New York	42.8
Paris	24.4
Rome	29.3
Sydney	46.5
Washington, D.C.	41.9

BOOK LINKS

- ***The Living Desert*** by Randy Moore and Darrell S. Vodopich (Enslow, 1991)
- ***A Living Desert*** by Guy Spencer (Troll, 1988)
- ***Deserts*** by Clive Catchpole (Dial, 1985)
- ***Lost in the Devil's Desert*** by Gloria Skurzynski (Morrow, 1993)

SPADEFOOT TOAD
KWL PATTERN

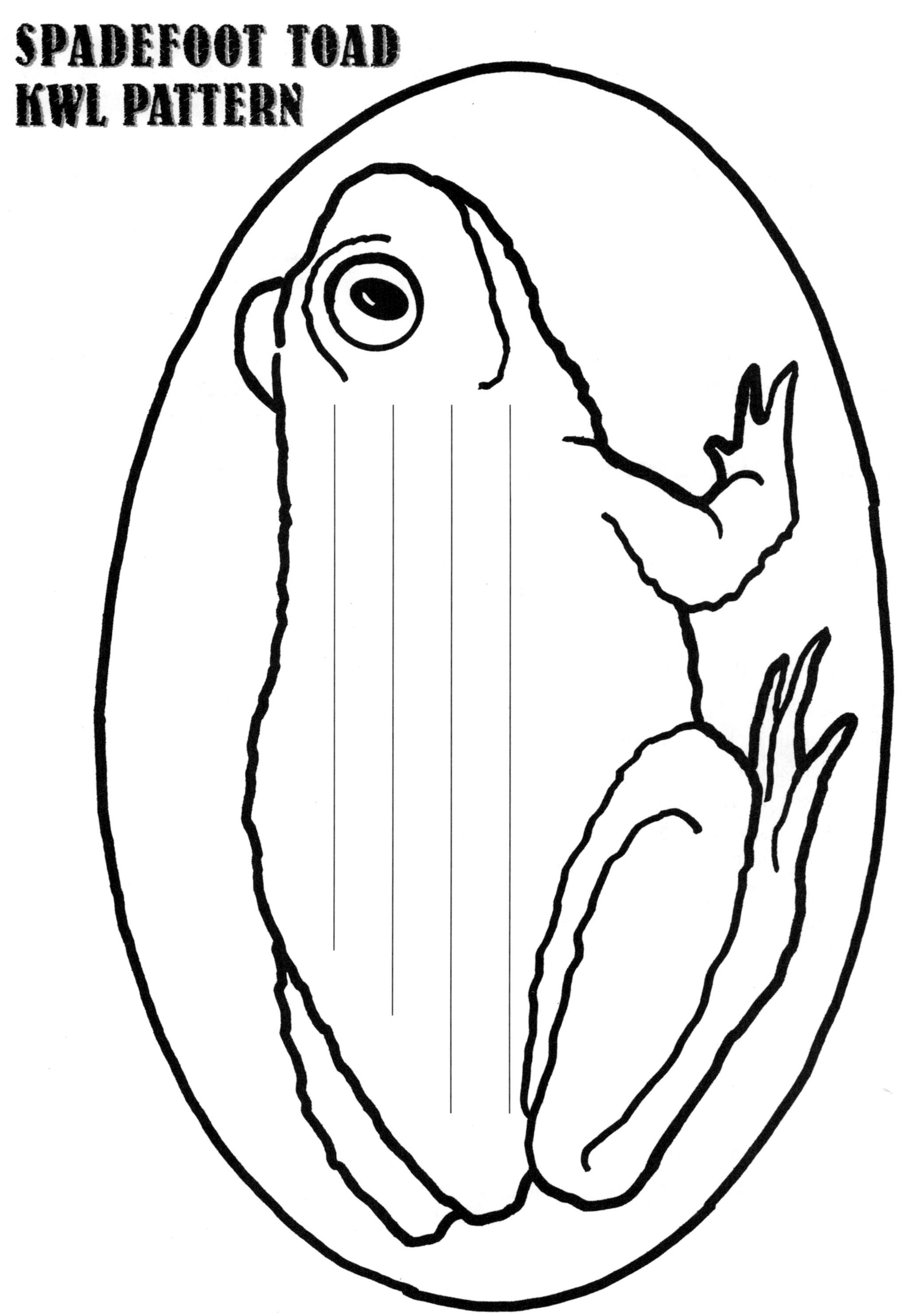

Name ______________________________

WHERE ARE THE DESERTS?

Use the poster map to answer these questions.

1. Which desert is about the same size as the United States?

____

2. Is there a desert in Canada? Is there one in Europe?

____

3. Find an inland desert. What's it called?

____

4. The Atacama Desert is in South America. Which coast is it on?

____

5. What kind of desert is the Namib?

____

6. The Sonoran Desert is in two countries. What are they?

____

7. Two of the smallest deserts are ______________________
and ______________________.

8. In which four states will you find the Great Basin Desert?

____

9. What kind of desert is the Great Basin?

____

10. Which desert is farthest south?

____

11. Which two deserts are farthest north?
______________________ and ______________________.

12. About what percentage of Australia is desert?

____

EXTRA: About what percentage of the Earth's land is desert? Estimate to find out.

 Name ______________________________

KING OF DESERTS QUIZ

What desert...

- is bigger than the United States?
- is home to 2 million people?
- has a name that means desert in Arabic?

Look at the map below and quiz yourself on the king of deserts!

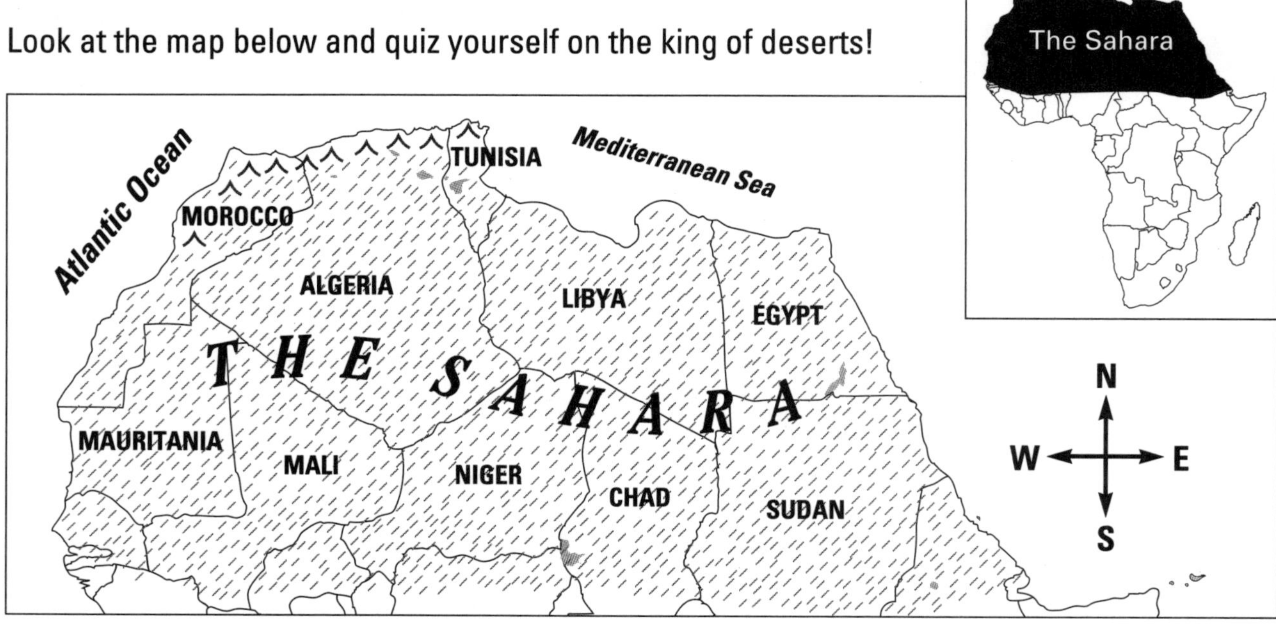

1. What's the name of this desert? ______________________________
2. What continent is it on? ______________________________
3. How many labeled countries are on the coast? ______________________________
4. Which two labeled countries are furthest from an ocean? ______________________________ and ______________________________
5. Which desert country is farthest north? ______________________________
6. Which three countries have mountains? ______________________________
7. What ocean is along the western coast? ______________________________
8. Write your own question. Then use the map to answer it. ______________________________

____

____

EXTRA: This desert is hot, dry, and full of dangerous sandstorms. How do people survive there? Use books to write a short report on how these desert people beat the heat.

Name ______________________________

RAIN, RAIN, COME AGAIN

Did you know that...

- *annual rainfall* means how much rain falls in a year.
- deserts get less than 10 inches of rain a year.
- when it does rain in a desert, it is often during a sudden storm. Then it may not rain again for years!

Here's a list of annual rainfall for eight desert cities. Fill in the amount of rain for each city on the bar graph on the following page. Then see which place is driest.

Antofagasta, Chile: $\frac{1}{2}$ inch	**Manama, Bahrain:** 3$\frac{1}{4}$ inches
Cairo, Egypt: 1 inches	**Phoenix, Arizona:** 6$\frac{1}{2}$ inches
Las Vegas, Nevada: 4 inches	**Ulan Bator, Mongolia:** 8 inches
Lima, Peru: 1$\frac{1}{2}$ inches	**Usakos, Namibia:** $\frac{3}{4}$ inches

After you've made your graph, answer the questions below.

1. Which desert city gets the most rain? ______________________
2. Which desert city gets the least rain? ______________________
3. How many of the cities get less than 5 inches of rain a year? ______________
4. How many cities get more than 5 inches of rain? ______________________
5. Would you like to live in a place that gets so little rain? Why or why not? __________

____

____

EXTRA: How much rain does your town get in a year? Where would it be on the bar graph above? Once you find out your town's annual rainfall, add it to the graph. (You may need to add paper!)

Name ______________________________

Antofagasta, Chile	Cairo, Egypt	Las Vegas, Nevada	Lima, Peru	Manama, Bahrain	Phoenix, Arizona	Ulan Bator, Mongolia	Usakos, Namibia

8
7
6
5
4
3
2
1
0

SCENIC SCULPTURE

Desert landscapes have been described in terms ranging from *bizarre* and *barren* to totally *breathtaking.* There's no autumn foliage or winter snow, crocuses don't herald spring, and the lush deep greens of summer never color the deserts. Yet desert landscapes are distinctive and varied. There are deep canyons, buttes, and columns in the southwestern United States; vast sand dunes in Arabia; more dunes and salt flats in the Sahara; and wind-sculpted *yardangs* (hillocks) in the Gobi.

Low annual rainfall is only part of what defines a desert. There's also an *annual evaporation rate,* or how much moisture evaporates from the surface per year. This is dependent on temperature, sunlight, and wind conditions. When the evaporation rate is higher than the annual rainfall of a specific area, that area is considered a desert—because it has a net deficit of water. Since most deserts are in high-pressure zones with little cloud cover, solar rays reach the desert floor and bounce back into the air as heat. The hot, dry air quickly evaporates any water on the ground. The forces of wind, water, and weathering are given more power by the high evaporation rate. Wind, for example, has sandblasting effects when dry sand, pebbles, and dirt are picked up. Moist soil, by contrast, is heavier and stays put.

BUTTE

Wind is one of the prime sculptors of desert terrain. Because of dry surfaces and little soil-anchoring vegetation, the wind—which really isn't any stronger than it is elsewhere—is simply more effective. It not only blows sand particles into high dunes, it then marches the huge sand masses across the land, progressing about 50 feet each year. In some parts of the Sahara, winds erode bedrock and carry away finer sand particles, leaving what's called a *reg*—closely packed pebbles made of less erodible material, like flint.

Water is an even more powerful erosive force than wind. Rainfall and riverflow are rare in desert areas. But when stream- and river-beds do fill with water, sediment is eroded and carried with enormous power. This mud, sand, and water slurry scours everything in it's path. It's how the Colorado River made the Grand Canyon.

ARCH

Weathering is how exposure to the elements breaks down rocks. It's a slower process, and a more subtle contributor to desert formations than wind and water, but it's just as important. Rock surfaces are severely affected by the extreme temperature variations; stones crack, chip, and shatter. Eventually the small pieces erode even more—

MESA

That's a Fact
Dunes on the Sahara can be over 800 feet high!

until they become the tiny granules we call sand. In America and Australia, weathering, combined with sudden fast-moving water and wind, formed towers and pillars.

STUDENT ACTIVITIES

Sandscapes

This is a group activity in which students create their own mini-desert landscapes. Each group needs a medium-sized rectangular cakepan, sand, assorted pebbles and stones, and straws.

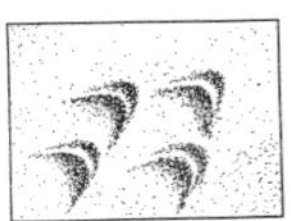

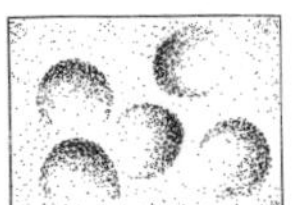

1. Copy and distribute the instructions on page 17 to each group.

2. Have children start out by making a fairly smooth desert with few characteristics. Typical dune patterns are illustrated, and the children can try to change their sandscapes by blowing through straws.

That's a Fact
Small whirlwinds called *dust devils* look like sand towers as they move across the desert floor.

EXTENSION ACTIVITY: Have a nitty-gritty discussion about sand, what it is, and how it's formed. You might also want to explain that the rock we call sandstone is hardened compressed sand from ancient inland seashores. Pass out pieces of medium-grit sandpaper for the children to handle. Have them use it on chalk, wood, and porous stones, and compare results. Ask: What would blowing sand do to desert structures?

Waterworks

In this three-part science experiment, students working in small groups will use their sandscapes to create their own desert terrain.

1. Copy and distribute pages 18 and 19 to each student. Although they'll work in teams, each child may participate in a different way, and therefore want to keep his or her own record.

2. Part One demonstrates how quickly rain evaporates in the desert.

3. Part Two illustrates gullies, *wadis*, and canyons. It shows children how they can make these desert shapes using water.

4. Part Three challenges students to form buttes, columns, and mesas using damp sand.

5. When the shapes have dried, kids may enjoy using more forceful streams of water, from a poultry baster, to produce arches.

EXTENSION ACTIVITY: Gather photographs of actual desert landscapes and formations (Death Valley, Bryce Canyon, and the Joshua Tree, for example). Challenge students to recreate these in their sand models. Ask: What desert conditions—rain, wind, and so on—could have created these formations?

Salt Flats

Salt flats and pans can be found on most deserts. They formed when large bodies of water repeatedly evaporated and left behind a residue of salt. Some salt pans, like our own Great Salt Lake, still have water. In other places, like the Dasht-e Kavir region of Iran, the ground is completely covered with a crust of salt. Explain that salt flats and pans are truly lifeless. Plants and crops can't grow in salt.

1. To show your class how a salt flat is formed, stir 5 tablespoons of table salt into 2 cups of warm water.
2. Pour the solution into a glass loaf pan.
3. Cut out the paper ruler below and tape it vertically to the side of the pan so kids can easily read the depth of the water. Place the pan on a sunny windowsill.
4. Ask a different group of children to check the pan each day. Have them use a highlighter to mark the water level each day. Do this until all the water evaporates. Then pass the pan around and ask: Where did the water go? What is the residue? (Touching it and tasting their fingers is a sure way to answer the question!)

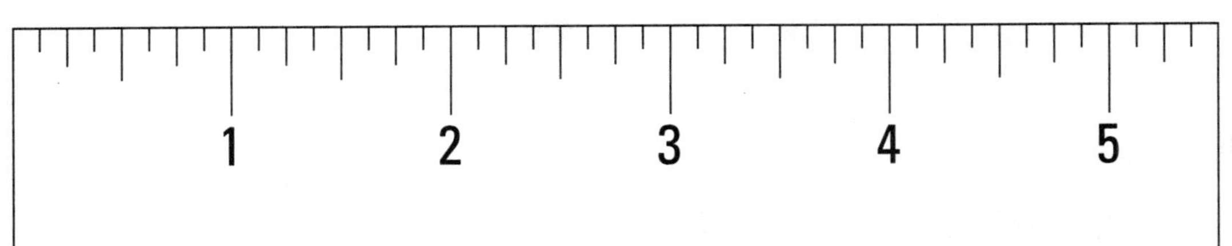

EXTENSION ACTIVITY: Make a salt lake by filling a pie pan with an inch or two of sand and covering it in the salt-water solution (see above). Set it in a sunny window. Have the students watch what happens as the water evaporates. Ask: What did the water leave behind? How does it compare to what real salt flats and pans look like? (Show photographs.) Older students might want to set up an experiment using different kinds of soils—sand, pebbles, clay—to observe the differences.

Evaporation

1. Start a discussion about evaporation. Ask the children where they think the water went in the Salt Flats experiment. When someone uses a blow-dryer on wet hair (or hands), what happens? Which do they think would dry something faster: heat, wind, or a combination of both? What kinds of experiments would help find out?

2. If your classroom chalkboard has a sunny area and a shaded one, try this: Have two students each use a wet sponge to write the word *water* one area at the same time. Have the class time the evaporation rate of both areas and discuss their observations.

EXTENSION ACTIVITY: Most blow-dryers have heat and air settings. Have the students design an experiment to find out how much faster water evaporates with wind and heat than just wind alone. Students could time the evaporation of a tablespoon of water in a bowl, for instance, using first the air and then the heat setting. Encourage them to make predictions first.

Sand-Art Paperweight

Using sand, some food coloring, and a small jar, your students can make attractive paperweights for themselves or as gifts for friends or relatives (see page 20).

EXTENSION ACTIVITY: Show examples of Navajo and Pueblo Indian sand-art designs to give students ideas. Ask: Where did they get colored sand thousands of years ago? (A photograph of the Painted Desert in Arizona shows magnificent layers of colored sediments—and answers the question.) Why do they paint in sand? (The paintings are often part of curing rituals.) Interested students could write a report about Native Americans sand art.

That's a Fact
Only about $\frac{1}{5}$ of the world's deserts are covered with sand.

BOOK LINKS

- ***A Desert Year*** by Carol Lerner (Morrow, 1991)
- ***When Clay Sings*** by Byrd Baylor (Macmillian, 1987)

Name(s) ______________________________

SANDSCAPES

You don't have to go to the desert to find out how sand dunes work. Just bury yourself in these instructions for making a mini-desert!

YOU WILL NEED:

- 1 rectangular cake pan (about 9-by-12-by-2 inches)
- newspapers
- drinking straw
- clean, fine sand
- large pebble

TO DO:

1. Put plenty of newspaper under the pan.
2. Carefully fill the cake pan half full with sand.
3. Gently shake the pan until the sand is even and smooth.

The sand-dune patterns below are found in deserts all over the world. Use wind (blowing through the straw) to make the same dune patterns in your sandscape.

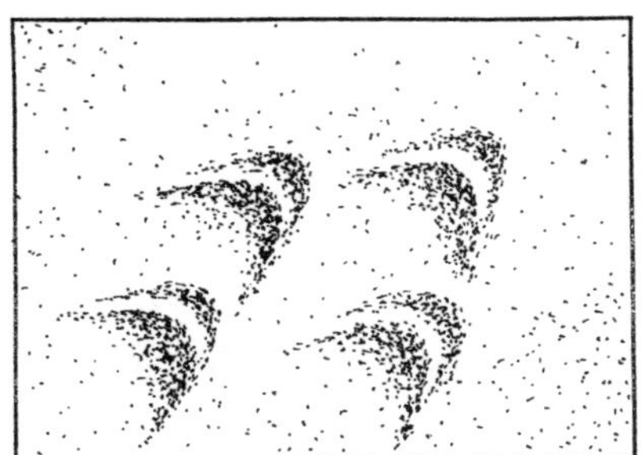

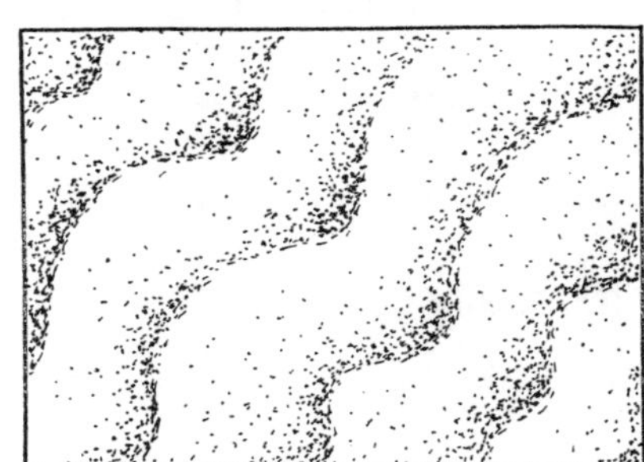

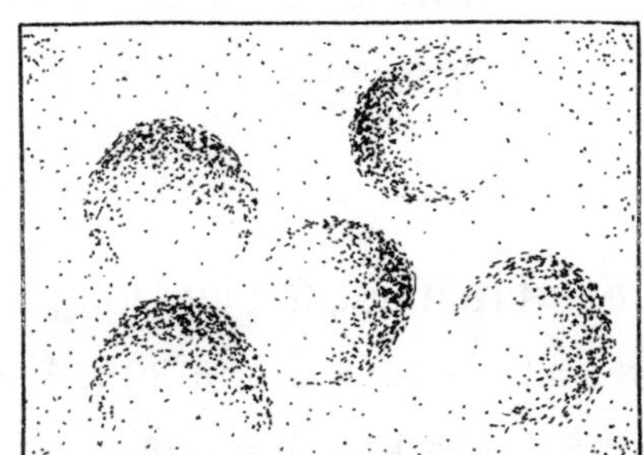

4. Now create three of your own sand patterns. Draw them below.

5. PEBBLE PUZZLE: Choose a sandy spot for the pebble. Push the pebble into the sand so only half of it shows. Now try to cover the pebble by blowing the sand around it. What works?

____

____

____

EXTRA: The Navajo and Pueblo Indians of the Southwestern United States paint pictures with sand. Use books to find out more about it.

Name ______________________________

WATERWORKS

There's not much water in a desert. But the water there helps shape the desert. Find out for yourself!

YOU WILL NEED:

- $\frac{1}{4}$ cup measuring scoop
- water
- your sandscape
- poultry baster or a big eyedropper
- sand
- water
- large paper cups
- salt shaker or small sprinkling can

TO DO:

1. Pour $\frac{1}{4}$ cup of water into a salt shaker or sprinkling can.
2. "Rain" the water on your desert.

   How long did it take for the water to soak in? ______________________

   What happened to the shape of the desert? ______________________

   ____

Desert rain doesn't last long. But it usually comes in a downpour! It can cut through the land like a bulldozer. Sometimes the rain makes a temporary steam, called a *wadi* (WAH-dee). Here's how to make one.

3. Make a shallow ditch from one end of your sandscape to the other by pressing the side of your hand in the sand.
4. Pour several cups of water into the wadi.

   How long does the water last? ______________________________

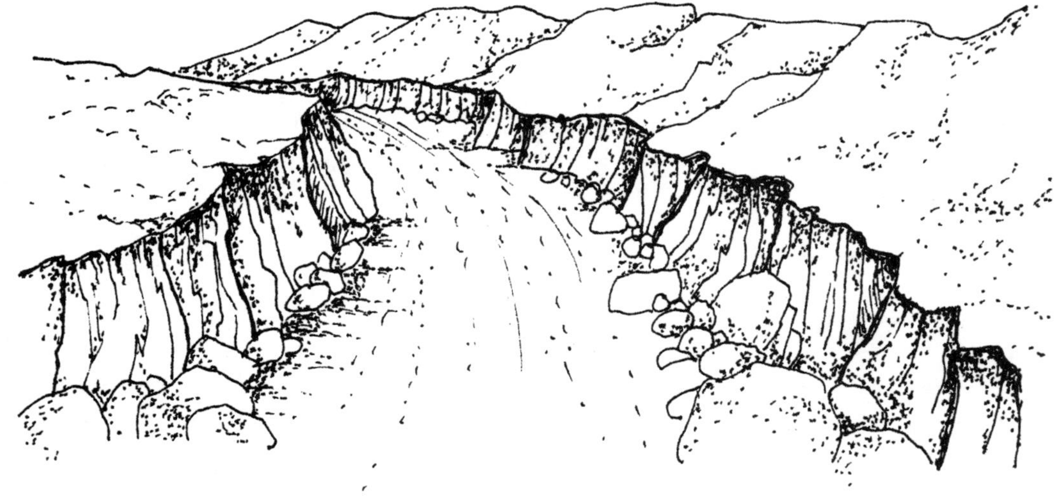

Take a look at the strange desert shapes in the three pictures below. Use some wet sand to make similar shapes with your hands.

COLUMN: First shape some flattened sand lumps out of damp (not drippy) sand. Make them different sizes. As you form each one, stack it on top of another, using a tiny bit of water to help them stick together.

BUTTE: This time make even flatter patty-like sand lumps. Layer them side by side on their ends.

MESA: First form a wide, low butte shape (see above). Next make the top perfectly flat. How? Get the top wet by sprinkling water on it. Then shave off the top with a piece of thin cardboard. (Hold it tightly on both ends while cutting.)

Put the shapes on your sandscape desert and let them dry.

Look at the arch below. Fast-running water carved it out of this desert tower.
Here's how to make one yourself:

ARCH: First make a column (see above) with a wide bottom. Then take aim with a baster full of water! Shoot water at a single spot near the bottom until it forms a little cave. Then shoot water from the back side until the cave opens into an arch.

Make and shape your own desert designs. Draw a picture of them here.

Name ____________________

SAND-ART PAPERWEIGHT

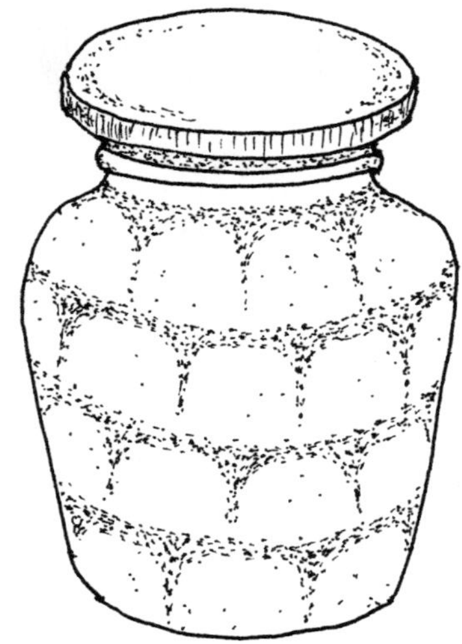

YOU WILL NEED:

- newspaper
- large paper cups
- fine sand
- plastic spoons
- food coloring
- small glass jar with lid
- thin paintbrush

TO DO:

1. Cover a desk or table with newspaper. Put the cups on the newspaper. You need one cup for each color.
2. Fill each cup about two-thirds full with sand.
3. Add 10 to 12 drops of a different food coloring to each cup. Mix well with the plastic spoons.
4. Let the sand dry. (Stirring it every few hours helps.)
5. Slowly pour some colored sand into the jar. Then pour a layer of another color. Keep layering until the jar is full of sand.
6. Now make designs! Slowly push the stem end of the paintbrush into the sand right alongside the glass. DO NOT STIR! Move it up and down in a few places inside the glass. As the stem goes down, different colors slide into the spaces, creating designs.
7. When you've finished making designs, fill the jar to the very top with sand.
8. Put the lid on tight. Now it's a paperweight!

EXTRA: The Navajo and Pueblo Indians of the Southwestern United States paint pictures with sand. Use books to find out more about it.

DESERT ANIMALS

Compared to animals who live in rain forests or savannahs, desert dwellers have a hard life. Food is scarce, temperatures are often high, there is little shade or protective cover, and most serious of all, there's little water. Yet hundreds of species—even fish—have developed the survival mechanisms needed to claim niches in this harsh environment. Some of their adaptations are common to wildlife everywhere—like camouflage and nocturnal activity. But other survival tactics belong to desert creatures alone.

That's a Fact
A scorpion can survive for a year without eating!

Creepy Crawlers

Because there aren't many small flying insects in the desert, most of the resident spiders are nocturnal ground hunters rather than web-spinners. Some of the large spiders are strong enough to capture lizards, rodents, and even small birds! Beetles do well in deserts because their waxy outer covering keeps moisture in. One beetle of the Namib fog desert has evolved an unusual strategy: It takes a head-down, bottom-up stance, so when the early morning fog condenses on its body, water runs down into its mouth! Some members of honeypot ant colonies become living storage tanks. Workers pass nectar and fruit juices to these honeypots ants, whose bodies grow to the size of peas. The engorged ants hang from the roof of the nest, and in the dry season, supply nectar to the colony.

Scales and Warts

Reptiles are somewhat able to control their body temperature through behavior. During the day they avoid lethal heat by burrowing in the sand or resting in dark crevices. Then at night, desert vipers with no sense of hearing and poor eyesight—like the diamondback rattlesnake—find prey using pits located between their nostrils and eyes. These odd sensors, smaller than the eyes and larger than nostrils, are heat-detecting organs. They detect infrared radiation and, therefore, perceive the presence of warm-blooded prey at a substantial distance. The sidewinder snake has developed a locomotion style that keeps most of its body off the hot ground. It thrusts its length forward at an angle to its travel direction, so its scales make brief contact with the sand at only two points.

That's a Fact
Millions of years ago, camels were the size of dogs.

Lizards are *diurnal* (day-active), although during the hottest seasons they limit their activity to early morning and evening. They've also evolved a range of beat-the-heat tactics. A bearded lizard runs on its hind legs to keep its body clear of the hot ground; the thorny devil drinks dew that forms on its dorsal spines; the gila monster stores food in its fat tail, and the chuckwalla spends most of each year in a dormant state known as *estivation*. All of the chuckwalla's body functions, including its heart rate, slow to nearly a full stop. In this flip side of hibernation, the animal is responding not to cold, but to heat and drought.

The spadefoot toads seem to live at two speeds: slow motion and fast forward. They spend ten inactive months a year in deep burrows. But the toads, like all amphibians, need water for breeding. When rain finally arrives, the toads rush to small temporary pools, breed, and lay their eggs. Tadpoles hatch in just two days and begin a race against time. They only need two weeks in the water to become tiny toads—but will the pool last that long?

Feisty Feathers

Some desert birds, like mourning doves and woodpeckers, can be found in many climates. Other species are strictly desert residents. One is the sparrow-sized elf owl, which makes its home in saguaro cacti. Another is the roadrunner, a tireless hunter of scorpions, lizards, and rattlesnakes. Ostriches also live in arid areas. Their thick plumage provides excellent protection against the sun, and their long eyelashes keep out sand. The sand grouse has a specialty that enables it to raise its family far from water: A fast flyer, a male grouse will make daily trips of 60 miles to find water. It saturates its breast feathers and returns to the nest, where the chicks drink the water from his spongy wet feathers.

That's a Fact
Chuckwallas sleep more than half of every year.

In the Company of Camels

Large grazing mammals have almost no chance of avoiding the heat, since there is little or no shade. To cope with the problem, the thick fur on their backs protects the skin beneath it. The underbelly, in shade, is nearly naked so that heat can escape. This is true of camels, addax, and other gazelles. Small desert mammals deal with heat simply by avoiding it! Almost all are nocturnal, and others emerge only in early morning or very late in the day. If a ground squirrel forages during the day, it flips its bushy tail over its head like an umbrella. Many carnivores and insect-eaters can live without ever drinking water, getting adequate moisture from their food.

STUDENT ACTIVITIES

Cool Critters

The 12 cards on pages 26 to 31 will help students better understand how different desert animals manage to survive. Reproduce and distribute the sheets, and have the children paste, cut, and assemble the cards. After they read the information on each card and look at the illustrations, ask: Which animals do you think are the most interesting? Why?

EXTENSION ACTIVITIES: The Cool Critter Cards can be used for more than just the activities below. Challenge students to come up with criteria for sorting the animals. For example, they can divide the cards into piles of diurnal and nocturnal animals; kinds of animals (bird, mammal, etc.); or herbivores, insectivores, omnivores, and carnivores.

That's a Fact
Kangaroos of the Australian deserts can cover 40 feet in one leap.

The animals could also be categorized by continent, and with some research—size or life span. A natural next step is to ask children to arrange three or four cards into a foodchain, reminding them to think about where animals live and what they eat. Have them compare their chains. (Example: wolf spider - elf owl - cacomistle, or jerboa - rattlesnake - roadrunner.)

Critter Spin!

The two spinner games on page 32 are based on information from the Cool Critter Cards.

1. After cutting out and assembling both spinners, divide the class into pairs of students.
2. Each pair lays out an entire set of cards between them. The cards need to be picture side up.
3. The object of the game is to collect the most cards.
4. **ROUND 1:** The Animal Names spinner is placed alongside the cards. Students take turns spinning and trying to match the name of the animal they land on to a picture on a card.
5. After choosing the card of the animal he or she thinks is correct, the student checks his or her answer by turning the card over. If it's the right animal, the student keeps the card. If it's wrong, the card is flipped back over. Note: If the spinner lands on an animal whose card is already taken, the player spins again. When the cards are all taken, the game's over. The player with the most cards wins.
6. **ROUND 2:** Change to the Animal Fast Facts spinner, replace the cards on the table and play again.

EXTENSION ACTIVITY: The game can be played in groups of three or four with more than one set of cards. The game can also be played with both spinners at once—players alternate spinners with each spin, or a card winner gets to tell the next person which spinner to use. Challenge groups of students to write—and play by—their own rules. Have students make their own fact-filled spinners.

That's a Fact
A jerboa's back legs are four times as long as its front legs.

Wizard Lizard

On pages 33 and 34 you will find directions and an easy four-piece pattern for making a stand-up frilled lizard puppet with moveable tail and frill.

1. After distributing copies of each page to your students, have them paste the pattern sheets to thin cardboard and color their lizards, using the Desert Animal Poster photo as a guide.
2. Help them cut and assemble their lizard puppets.
3. Explain that this Australian lizard is a good bluffer. When it's frightened, it puts up its umbrella-like frill and instantly looks much bigger. As it displays its frill, it also makes a loud hissing sound. The whole act usually works well enough to frighten away enemies.
4. Using their sandscapes as habitats, the children can have their lizards meet on the sand, display their frills and hiss as they act out parts in the play on page 36.

EXTENSION ACTIVITY: Students can find out more about the Australian frilled lizard in the library.

Dasher the Dingo

The dingo puppet on page 35 can be used by itself or with the Wizard Lizard puppets in the Fearsome Foursome play on page 36.

1. Make a copy of the pattern for each student.
2. Ask them to color the dingo, paste it to thin cardboard, then cut it out.
3. Tape the holding tab to the back to give children something to grasp while moving the puppet.

EXTENSION ACTIVITY: Dingoes have been companions of Australia's aboriginal people for thousands of years. In fact, dingoes were probably brought to Australia when the aborigines migrated to the island continent 40,000 years ago. (Humans, dingoes, and bats were the only native non-marsupial mammals in Australia before European settlers came.) Challenge students to find out more about the dingo's role in aboriginal life.

That's a Fact
A jackrabbit can walk soon after it's born.

Fearsome Foursome

Fearsome Foursome is a short rhyming play about four frilled lizards who stop their show-off competition long enough to outwit a dingo. Each student should have a copy of the play on page 36. Students can read the parts, or use the Wizard Lizard and Dasher the Dingo puppets to act out the play on their sandscapes.

EXTENSION ACTIVITIES: After children have read their parts, ask them to draw a picture about the story. Groups of students can also brainstorm and write their own desert dramas, even creating their own desert animal puppets and characters.

Desert Dominoes

1. Each domino on pages 37 and 38 has two desert animals pictured end to end. Reproduce and distribute the sheets, and ask children to paste the sheets onto oaktag or cardboard. (One complete set of dominoes is necessary for each pair of players.)
2. Have them color the animal pictures, and then cut out the domino shapes. Review what the different domino animal categories are: mammals, birds, reptiles, and arthropods. They need to understand these categories to play.
3. The game begins with all dominoes turned picture side down. Each child picks and keeps four dominoes but doesn't show them to her or his opponent.
4. Spin a pencil or flip a penny to see who goes first.

5. Player A lays a domino on the table, picture side up.
6. In order to lay out a card, player B must be able to put mammal to mammal, bird to bird, arthropod to arthropod, or reptile to reptile. If B can't do that, he or she must draw from the board until a domino that can be played is drawn.
7. Players alternate turns, and whoever gets rids of all his or her dominoes first is the winner. If, at the end, neither child can play their remaining dominoes, the one with the fewest dominoes left is the winner.

That's a Fact
A fennec is only about 15 inches long—but its ears are 6 inches long!

Research Report

1. Divide the class into research teams of three or four students.
2. Ask each team to select an animal from the Desert Animals poster or from Desert Dominoes. Have them announce their selection so there's no duplication. (You might suggest that they have a second-choice animal in mind.)
3. Challenge the teams to find information about their animal from magazines and reference books. Make enough copies of the Research Report on page 39 for each team. When they've completed their investigation, have them fill in the information.

EXTENSION ACTIVITY: Ask students to present their information to the class. Their presentations could be accompanied by maps showing where the animals live.

Animal Alphabet

1. Help the students lightly draw a large block letter of their first or last name initial. Explain that they're going to draw a picture of a desert animal and/or plant that begins with the same letter. Show them the sample below based on the letter *C*.
2. Help them find models for their artwork on the poster, Critter Cards, or Animal Dominoes.
3. After the animal or plant is drawn, ask them to color the block letter. They may also enjoy adding some background desert details.
4. Display the desert alphabet while the unit is being studied.

BOOK LINKS

- ***Desert Voices*** by Bryd Baylor (Macmillian, 1981)
- ***Day and Night in the Desert*** by Jennifer O. Dewey (Little, 1991)

SPADEFOOT TOAD

Animal type: amphibian
When it's active: night
Its home: southwestern United States
Its food: insects

FAST FACTS:

- A spadefoot can disappear in seconds. It digs backwards into sandy soil with its hard-edged hind feet.
- This toad sleeps for 10 months each year!
- Spadefoots wake up when it rains. They rush to breed and lay eggs in puddles.
- Tadpoles hatch after only two days. Two weeks later, the tadpoles are tiny toads.

ROADRUNNER

Animal type: bird
When it's active: day
Its home: southwestern United States
Its food: insects, scorpions, snakes

FAST FACTS:

- A roadrunner rarely flies, but it can run 30 miles per hour!
- It builds its nest in the safety of a cactus bush.
- The roadrunner can kill a rattlesnake!
- It cracks open desert snails by hitting them against rocks.
- This noisy bird coos, crows, clacks, and chuckles.

HORNED TOAD

Animal type: reptile
When it's active: day
Its home: southwestern United States
Its food: insects

FAST FACTS:

- The horned toad is really a lizard!
- It buries itself under the sand, leaving only its head out. When ants march by, it sweeps them in with a flick of its tongue.
- Predators usually don't bother it because of its spines and awful taste.
- When really excited, the horned toad sprays blood from the corners of its eyes!

FENNEC

Animal Type: mammal
When it's active: night
Its home: Africa
Its food: locusts, lizards, mice

FAST FACTS:

- This is the smallest fox in the world, but it has the biggest ears!
- Its ears can hear even the faintest sounds. They also help keep the fennec cool by giving off heat.
- Hairy soles on its feet help this desert fox run on sand.
- A fennec doesn't need to drink water. It gets enough moisture from its food.

JERBOA

Animal type: mammal
When it's active: night
Its home: Africa and Asia
Its food: insects, seeds

FAST FACTS:

- A jerboa's hind legs are four times longer than its front ones.
- This tiny rodent can jump 15 feet in one hop!
- A jerboa can dig down 6 feet—the deeper, the cooler.
- During the hottest part of the summer, it closes the entrance to its den to keep moisture in and heat out.
- A jerboa doesn't drink water. It gets water from its food.

RATTLESNAKE

Animal type: reptile
When it's active: night
Its home: United States
Its food: lizards, rodents, small mammals

FAST FACTS:

- A rattlesnake doesn't lay eggs like most snakes. It gives birth to live young.
- It shakes the rattle on its tail as a warning to keep away.
- Each time a rattlesnake changes its skin, it gets a new ring on its rattle.
- When hunting in the dark, pits near the rattlesnake's eyes sense the heat of a nearby animal.
- Like other snakes, a rattler on the prowl flicks its tongue. It's tasting the air for danger and food.

PECCARY

Animal type: mammal
When it's active: day
Its home: southwestern United States and Mexico
Its food: roots, grass, tubers, cacti

FAST FACTS:

- The peccary can eat a cactus, spines and all!
- It marks its territory with smelly musk from a gland on its back.
- Razor-sharp tusks are its defense weapons.
- Females give birth to twins. They can outrun a person when they're only three hours old!

ELF OWL

Animal type: bird
When it's active: night
Its home: southwestern United States
Its food: scorpions, spiders, insects

FAST FACTS:

- The elf owl is only five inches long—the size of a sparrow!
- It hears well, has super eyesight, and flies without making a sound.
- Elf owls nest in old woodpecker holes in cacti. The cactus spines protect it from hungry predators.
- Nests in the cacti stay cool. Why? The plant's thick covering stores moisture.

WOLF SPIDER

Animal type: arachnid
When it's active: night
Its home: southwestern United States
Its food: insects

FAST FACTS:

- Instead of catching insects in webs, this fast-moving spider catches its prey on the ground.
- It has excellent eyesight...and eight eyes!
- The mother spider weaves a sac around her eggs. Then she attaches it to her abdomen.
- When the spiderlings hatch, they climb onto their mother and ride on her back.

AFRICAN BLACK-FOOTED CAT

Animal type: mammal
When it's active: night
Its home: southwestern Africa
Its food: birds, rodents, lizards, insects

FAST FACTS:

- This is the smallest of all cats. It makes a housecat look like a giant!
- It has large ears and a tan coat with dark spots.
- The black-footed cat has strong front paws. It uses them to dig up hiding lizards, rodents, and insects.
- It's often called the *ant hill tiger* because it spends the days in old termite mounds.

COOL CRITTER CARDS

CACOMISTLE

Animal type: mammal
When it's active: night
Its home: southwestern United States and Mexico
Its food: plants, birds, rodents, insects

FAST FACTS:

- Often called *ringtailed cat,* the cacomistle is really a raccoon relative.
- When threatened, it spits like a cat, but it also barks like a dog!
- The cacomistle's bushy tail is longer than its body!
- Early settlers in the Southwest kept them as pets because they were affectionate and caught rodents.

PACK RAT

Animal type: mammal
When it's active: night
Its home: southwestern United States
Its food: cactus stems, fruit, insects

FAST FACTS:

- A pack rat really isn't a rat—it belongs to a different group of rodents, called *voles.*
- It collects all kinds of things—especially bright objects—and packs them in its nest.
- It builds its den in clumps of cactus and carpets it with grass.
- A pack rat gets all the water it needs from its food.

CRITTER SPIN

Get in the spin of things with this fun spinner game!

YOU WILL NEED:

- scissors
- brass fasteners
- paper clips

TO DO:

1. Cut out each spinner.
2. Open a paper clip so it makes an *S* shape.
3. Push a brass fastener through the black dot in the center of the spinner.
4. Hook one end of the opened paper clip around the fastener (see picture).
5. Turn the spinner over and bend back the fastener ends.
6. Test it! The paper clip needs to be loose enough to spin, but not so loose it flies off.

Assembled Spinner

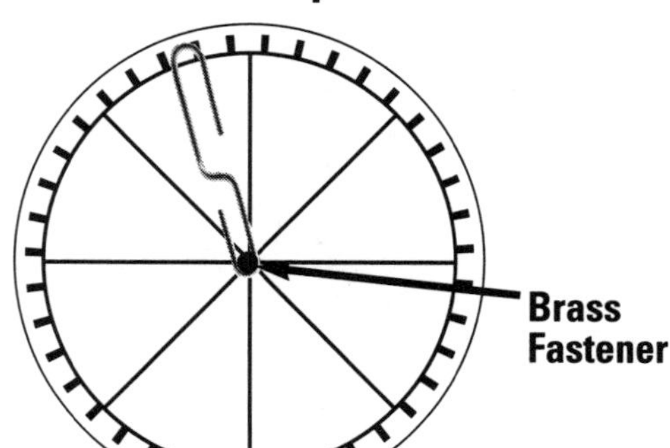

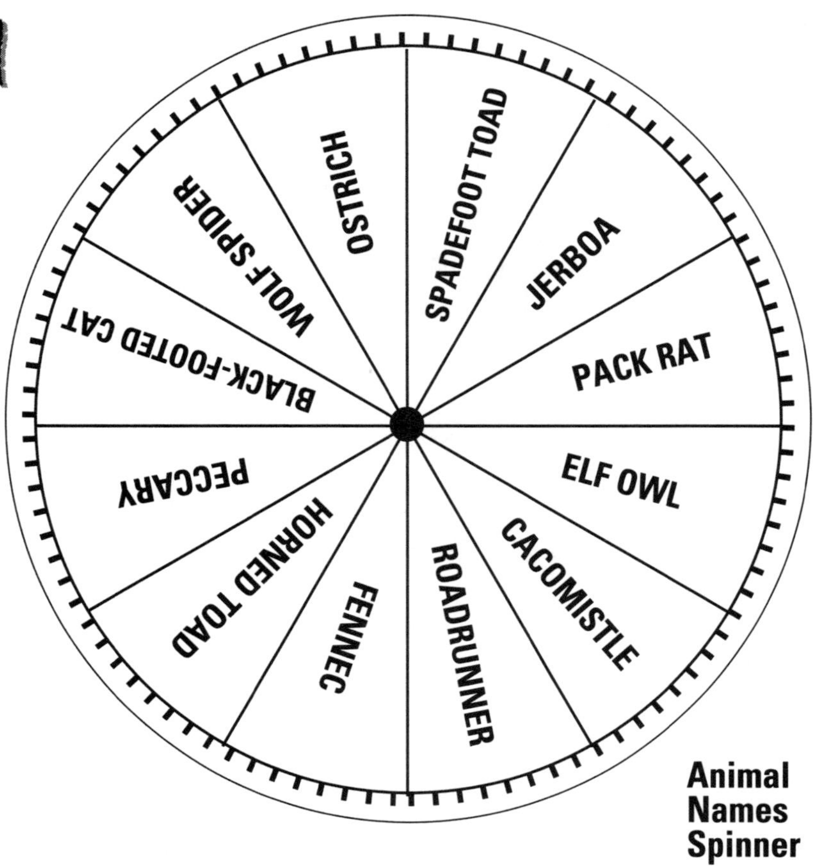

Animal Names Spinner

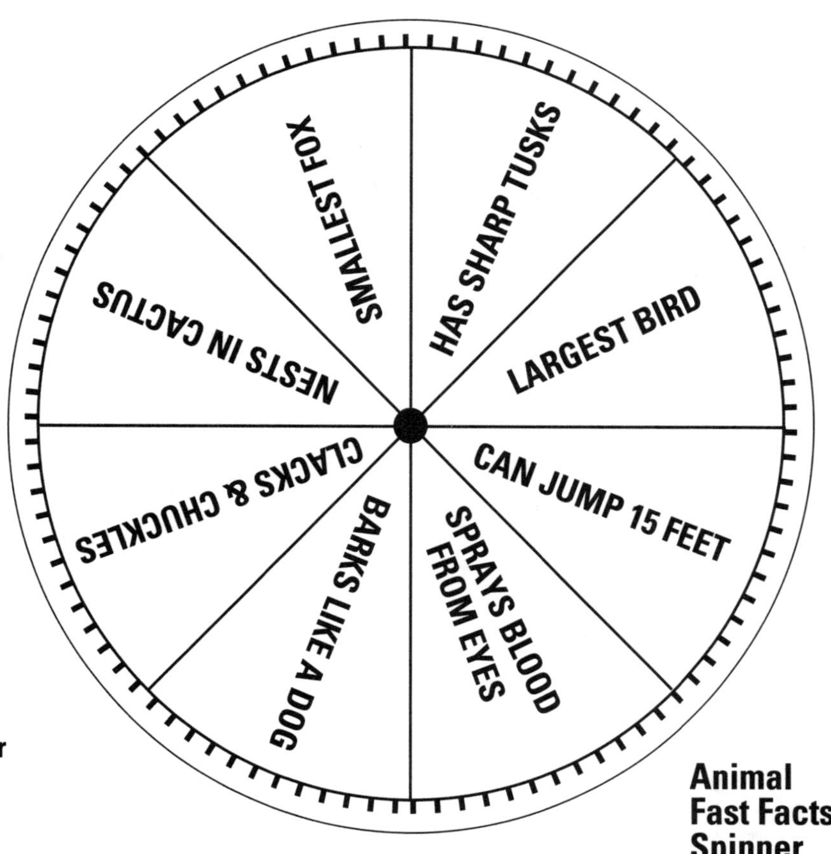

Animal Fast Facts Spinner

MAKE A WIZARD LIZARD

The Australian frilled lizard is a wizard at fooling predators. Find out how it does it by putting together this puppet.

YOU WILL NEED:

- Wizard Lizard pattern
- crayons or markers
- paste
- cardboard or oaktag
- tape

TO DO:

1. Cut out the frilled collar pattern and set it aside.
2. Paste the rest of the page to cardboard or oaktag.
3. Color the pieces, including the frill. (You can color it like the frilled lizard on the Desert Animals poster, or differently.)
4. Carefully cut out all the pieces.
5. Fold the thick end of the tail along the dotted line to form a handle.
6. Tape the holding tab to the back of the lizard.
7. Slip the tail through the holding tab, pointy end first.
8. To make the lizard stand up, fold along the dotted line under the rocks.
9. Fold the frill collar in half and snip along the line. Then fold it in half again. Open it and carefully slip it over the lizard's head.

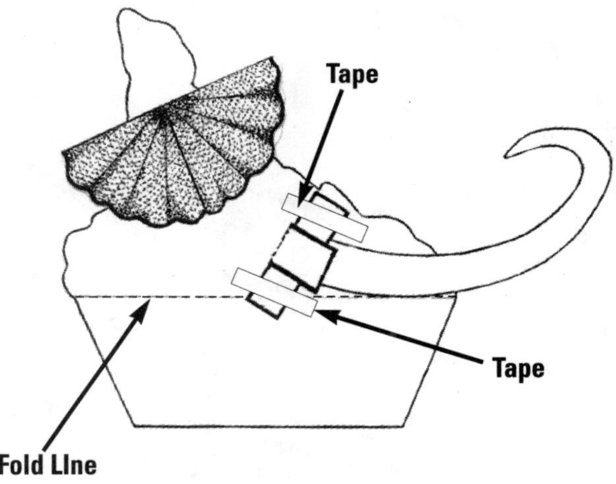

When your Lizard is sunning himself, he looks like this:

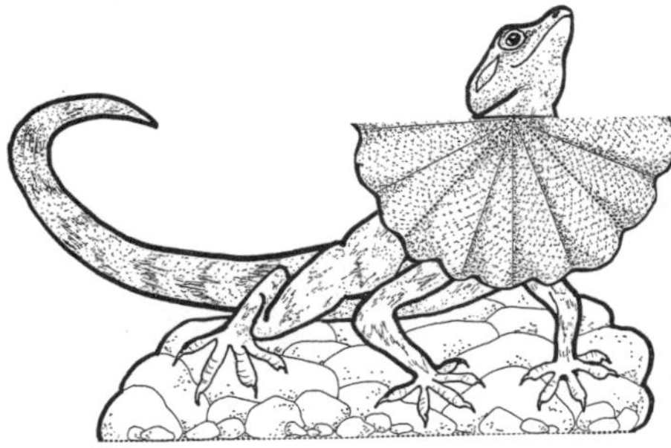

When he wants to scare away a predator, his frill goes up. (You can put it up for him.)
Then he flicks his tails up and down. (Move the tail handle for him.) He looks like this:

WIZARD LIZARD PATTERN

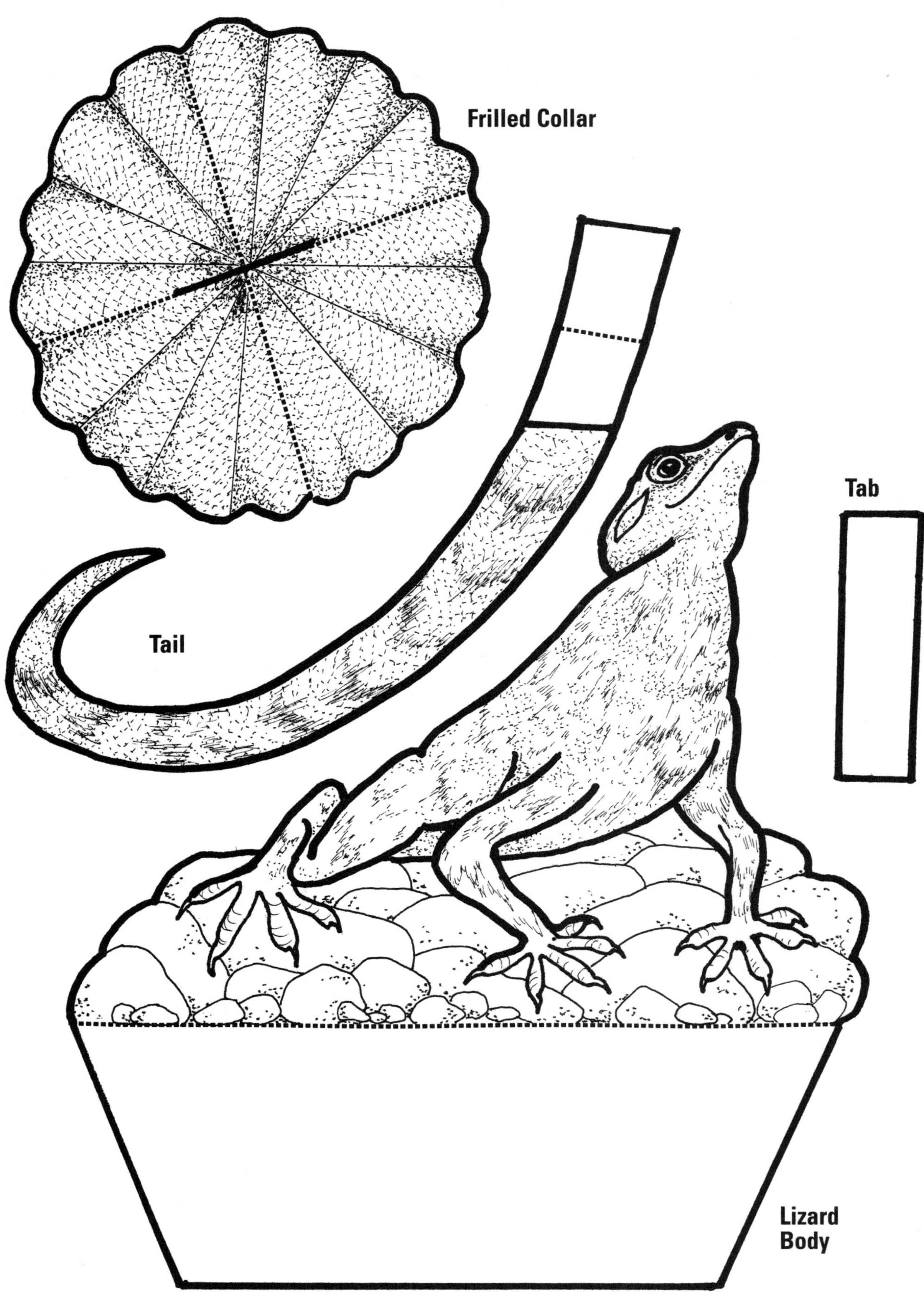

DASHER THE DINGO PATTERN

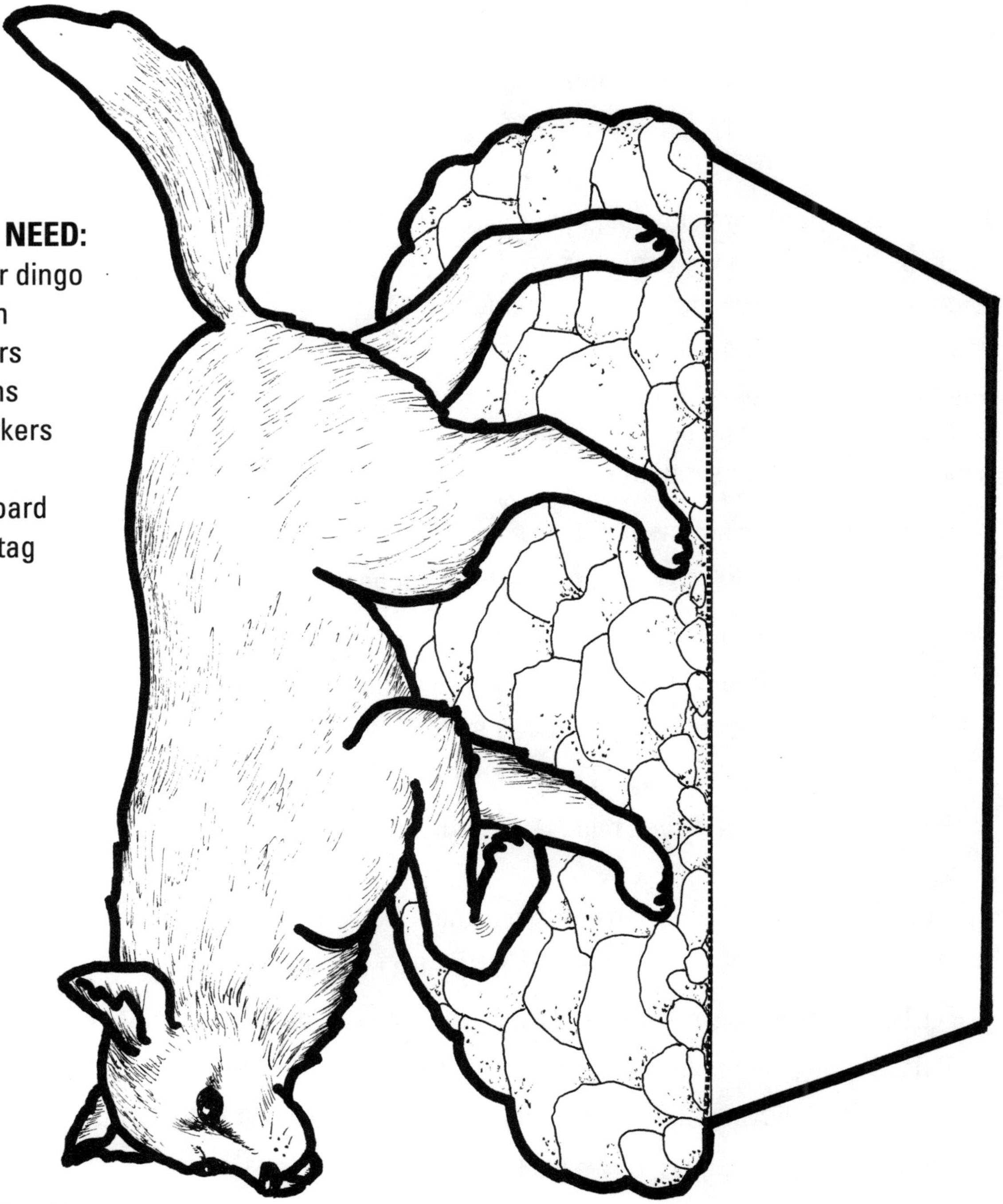

YOU WILL NEED:

- Dasher dingo pattern
- scissors
- crayons or markers
- paste
- cardboard or oaktag
- tape

TO DO:

1. Color the dingo.
2. Paste the page to cardboard or oak tag.

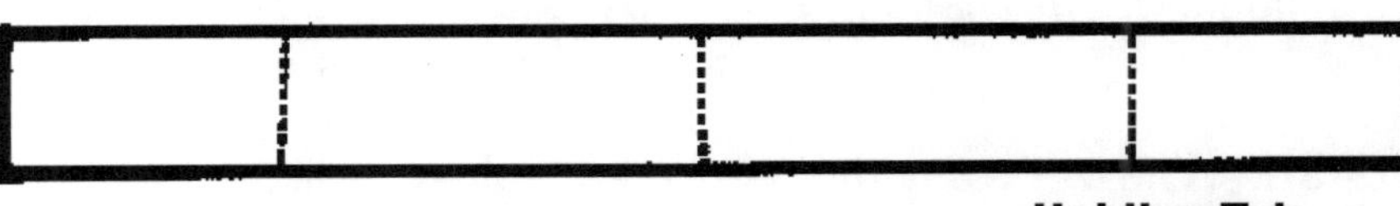

Holding Tab

3. Carefully cut both pieces out. (Watch the tail!)
4. Fold along dotted line to make Dasher stand up.
5. Bend the Holding Tab into a C shape and tape both tab ends onto the dingo's back. This is a handle for you to hold.

FEARSOME FOURSOME

CAST:

- four frilled lizards: Flash, Fletch, Flip, and Fancy
- one dangerous dingo: Dasher

SCENE: The lizards are standing in a circle on the sand, facing one another. Each is trying to prove that he or she is the best and most fearsome lizard of all. They compete by lifting their frills, whipping their tails, hissing—and boasting. (Your sandscape is a perfect setting.)

FLASH: *(admiring her own tail)* My tail is surely the longest.

FLETCH: Maybe that's so, but mine is the strongest!

FLIP: That doesn't matter, guys. My tail is roughest.

FANCY: What good is that? My tail is toughest.

FLASH: Who wants to race? I can run fast!

FLETCH: Last time we raced, Flash, you came in last!

FLIP: *(hisses)* What do you think? Do I sound like a snake?

FANCY: Snakes out here rattle, so you sound like a fake.

FLASH: *(raising her frill for a moment)* Hey, isn't this a scary sight?

FLETCH: *(raising his frill for a moment)* Now mine could give you quite a fright!

FLIP: *(raising his frill for a moment)* I declare my frill the winner!

(DASHER APPEARS, SLOWLY MOVING CLOSER, STALKING THE LIZARDS.)

FANCY: Watch out, guys, or we'll all be dinner!

(The four lizards huddle together. Then, just as dasher rushes at them, all four frills go up at once, and they all hiss loudly. The dingo stops in his tracks. Then he turns and runs away. When he's gone, the lizards flop down with relief)

FLASH: Whew! I'd say that was a very close call...

FLETCH: Not when it's all for one, and one for all.

FLIP: All together, we were awesome!

FANCY: Hooray for us, the Fearsome Foursome!

DESERT DOMINOES

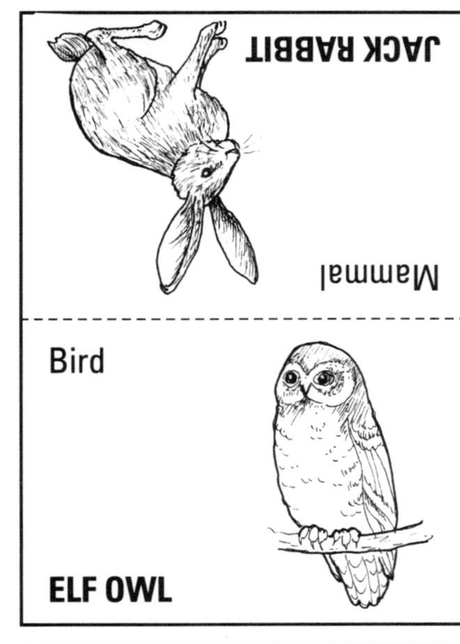

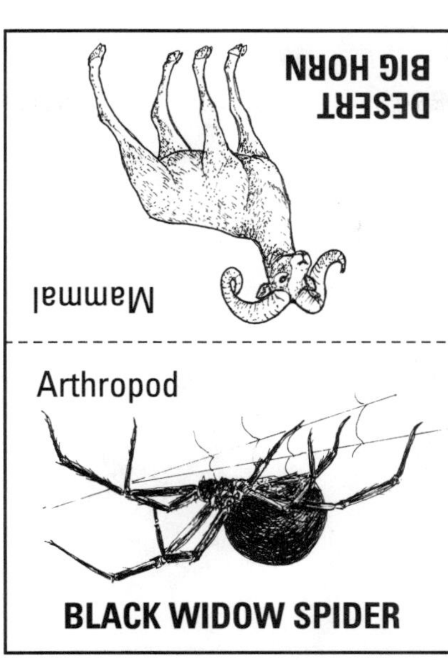

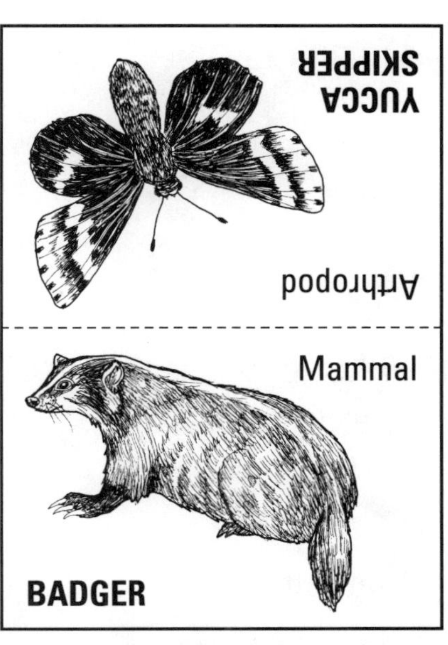

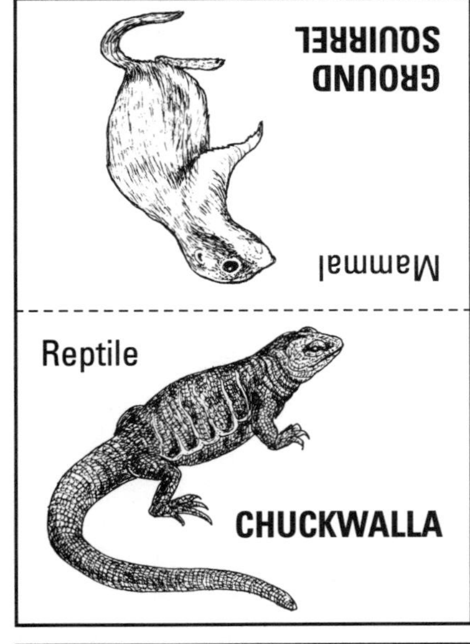

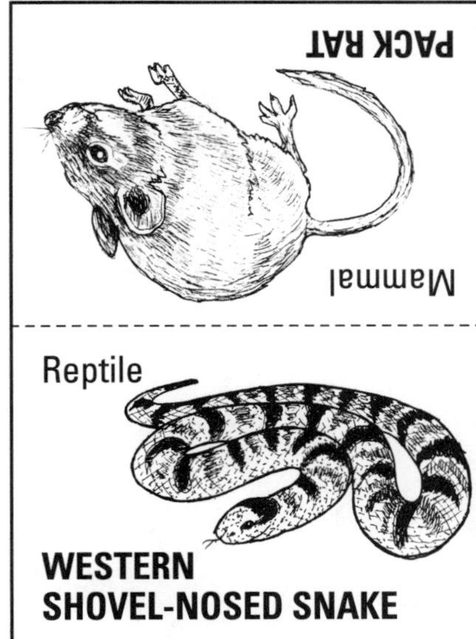

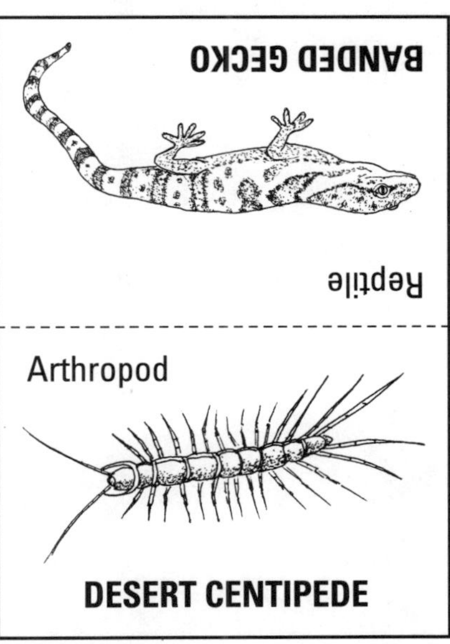

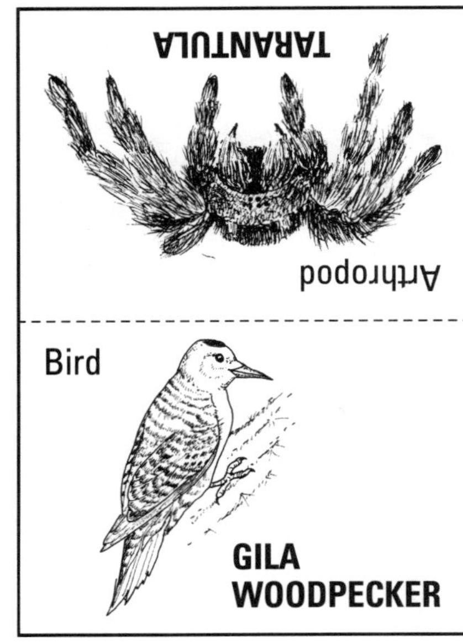

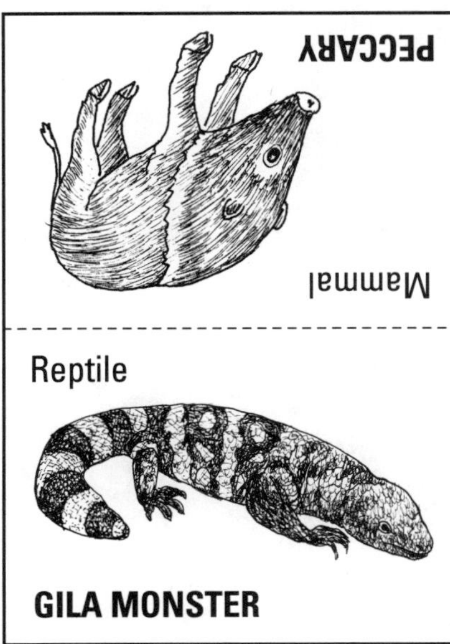

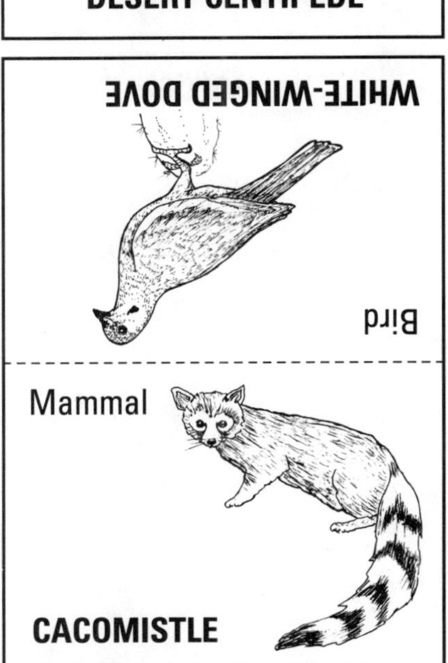

DESERT DOMINOES

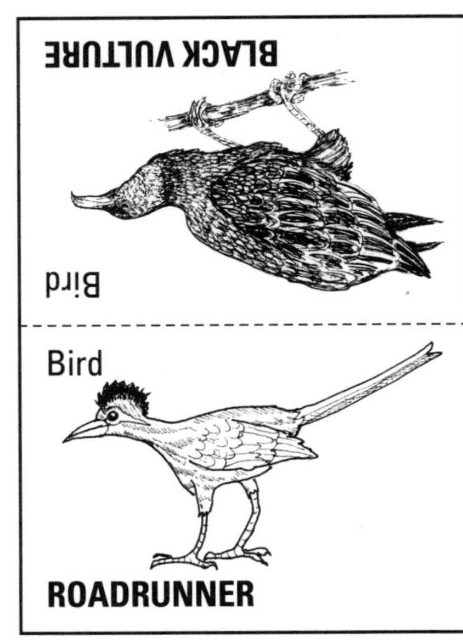

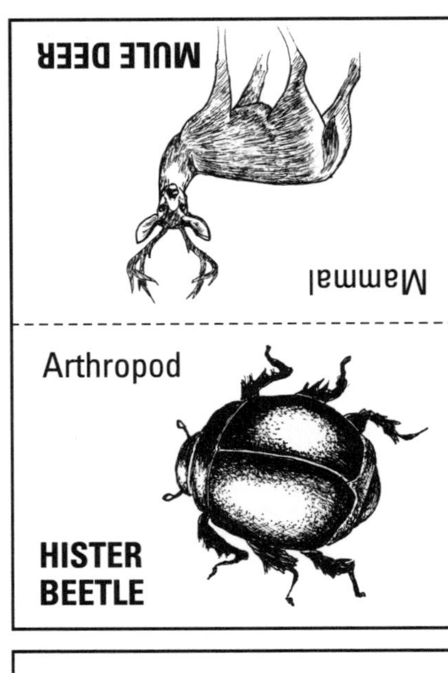

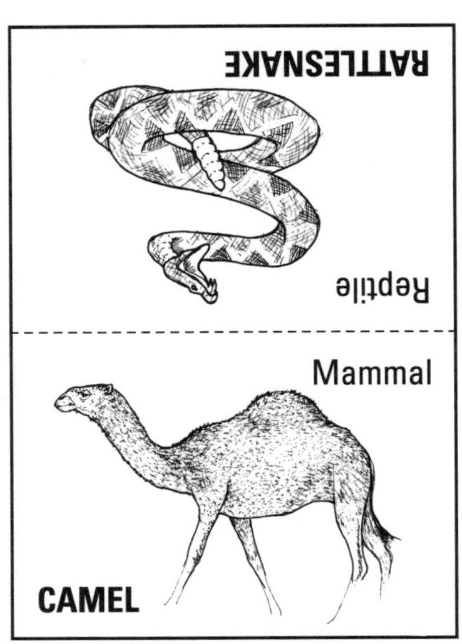

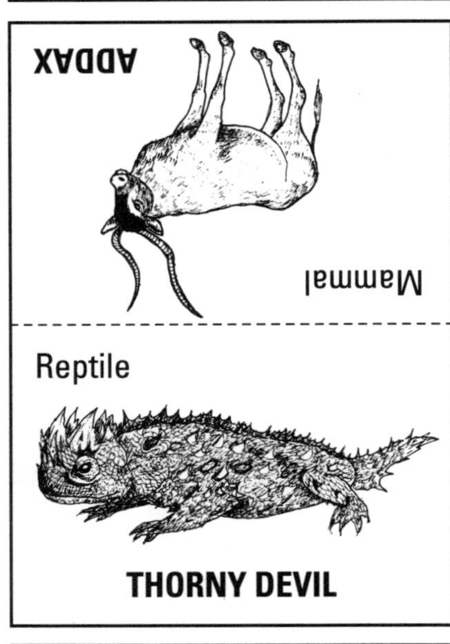

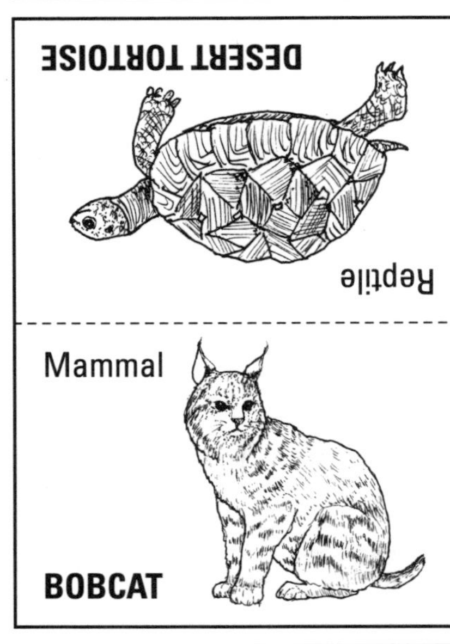

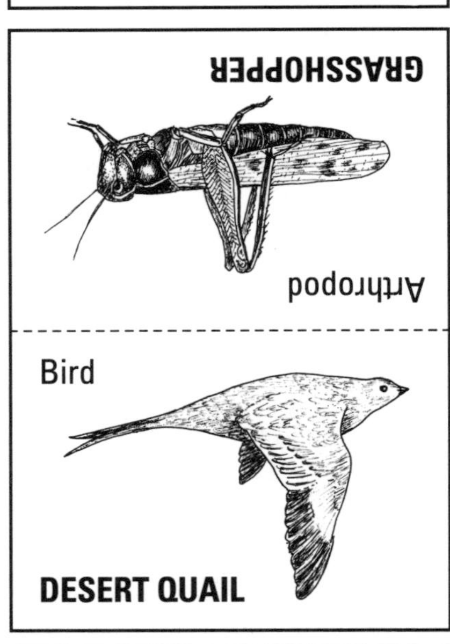

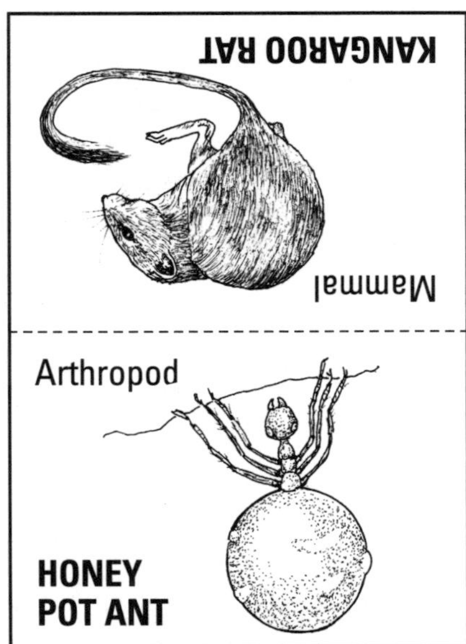

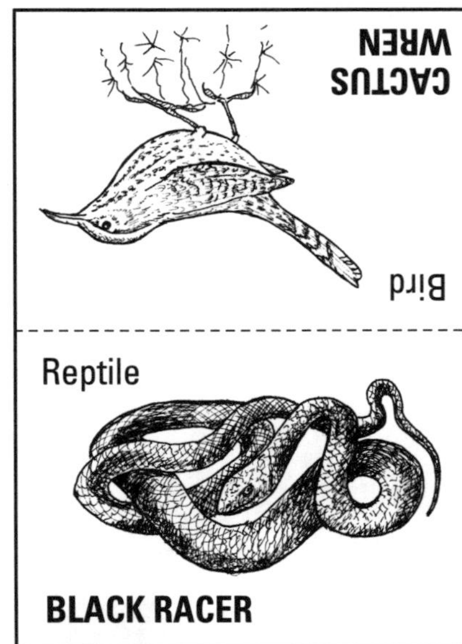

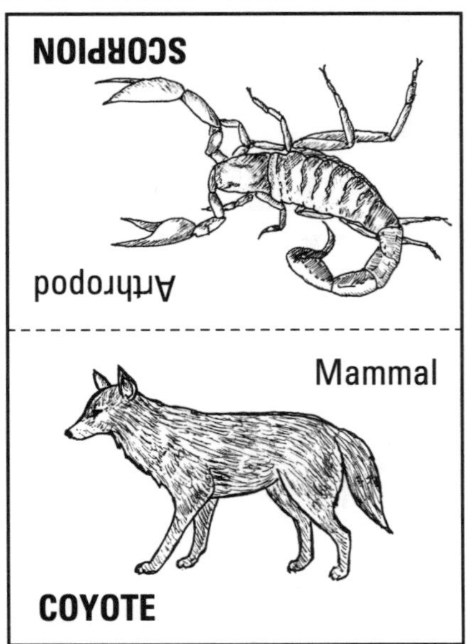

Name(s) ____________________

DESERT ANIMAL DATA SHEET

What is this animal called? ____________________

What type of animal is it? ____________________

How big is it? ____________________

Where does it live? ____________________

What does it eat? ____________________

When is it most active
(day, night, morning, or evening)? ____________________

How does it beat the heat? ____________________

____

What really neat things can it do? ____________________

____

Draw a picture of it:

EXTRA: Does this desert animal remind you of an animal that doesn't live in the desert? Which one?

PRICKLY PLANTS

Desert animals may resemble their relatives in other parts of the world, but desert plants have no such look-alikes. From seeds to leaves to roots, they're unique. Even the basic process of photosynthesis is different. All plants need to open their pores *(stomata)* in order to absorb carbon dioxide and release oxygen. But when they do this, moisture is lost. In temperate climates this moisture loss (called *transpiration*) isn't a problem because more water is simply taken up by the roots. In a desert, however, water is scarce and plant survival depends on some very unusual water-conserving adaptations. The plants in arid areas have fewer and smaller stomata than their temperate or tropical counterparts. Some drought-resistant and succulent plants have further adapted by not opening their stomata during the heat of the day at all. They wait until after sundown to open their stomata and absorb carbon dioxide. The plants then store the carbon dioxide until the next day's sunlight starts photosynthesis, while the stomata remain closed.

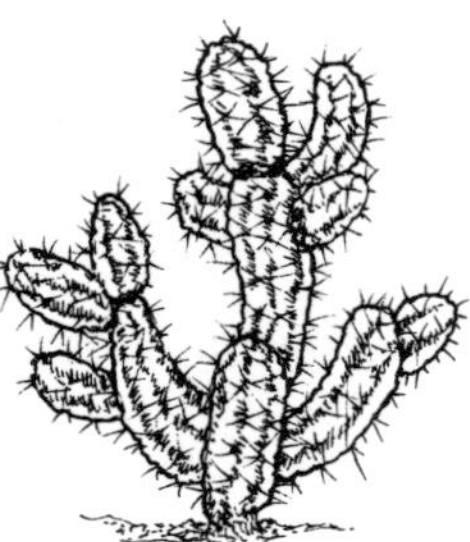

Since moisture evaporates from surfaces exposed to the sun, some desert plants have very small leaves, some roll up their leaves during the hottest part of the day, and still others have no leaves at all! Many are *drought-deciduous*; that is, they sprout leaves only during the rainy season, and drop them when it gets dry.

In addition to saving water by reducing transpiration, desert succulents store water in their fleshy leaves. The accordion pleats in many cacti expand with water taken up when it rains. The cactus stores the water for use during the long dry spells. Desert plants take up water in several ways. The roots of some desert shrubs and plants are often extremely deep and able to tap into water 50 to 100 feet below the ground. Others have a wide network of roots just below the surface, which can more easily catch water from dew and an occasional shower. Some plants have *both* deep taproots and a shallow root network. The strange star-shaped latifolia from the Atacama desert has no roots at all! Its stiff leaves form a ball that is blown by the wind.

Playing Dead

Some plants dry up and die above ground during extreme heat, but they're not really dead. Water stored in the roots sustains them until the next rain, when they send up new growth. Flowers also make brief appearances on deserts. After a hard downpour, a profusion of flowers may appear in a sudden burst of color. But with none of the prickly plants' coping abilities, they soon fade, go to seed, and are gone. The seeds they leave behind are coated with chemical inhibitors that prevents germination until rain washes them away—and that may be a very long time. Scientists at an archaeological site found 300-year-old "sleeping" seeds that were still able to germinate!

STUDENT ACTIVITIES

Cactus Cube Toss

> **That's a Fact**
> **In one day, a fruit tree can lose more than 300 quarts of water, while a large saguaro loses less than a cup of water.**

1. Copy and distribute copies of the cactus cube patterns on page 44 to each child.
2. Paste the pages to light colored construction paper.
3. Have children cut them out and fold along all the dotted lines. They can color them before folding.
4. Show children how to form the pattern into a cube by tucking in all the blank sections. You might suggest taping the edges so the cubes don't come apart during play.
5. Cactus Cube Toss is played by two students, each with a Cactus Cube One cube (it has six *different* cacti sides). The object is to collect ten points.
6. The game begins when player A tosses a cube onto a flat surface.
7. Player B gets three chances to roll a matching picture with his or her own cube. A cacti match earns one point. If B fails to get a match in three tries, player A gets the point.
8. The next round begins with B rolling a cube and A trying to match it. Play continues until one of the players reaches the winning score of 10 points.

EXTENSION ACTIVITY: Point out that some cacti have very descriptive names. Ask students if they think the plants pictured on the cubes are well named. Can they think of other names for them? On the board, list the names of some other desert plants, such as: strawberry cactus, elephant tree, ice plant, pincushion cactus, feather cactus, sand dollars, pencil cholla, beavertails, hedgehog cactus, and baby toes. Challenge students to draw what they think those plants look like. They may also enjoy drawing and naming an imaginary cactus of their own. Collect the pictures into a class book of Creative Cacti. Then share pictures of the actual plants with students. How do the children's interpretations compare?

Prickly Probabality

1. Review simple probability with your students. Ask: If I flip a penny 30 times, about how many times will be heads and about how many times tails? What about throwing a die? About how many times will the number six come up out of 30 throws?
2. As a class, test this with Cactus Cube One. Six students can keep tallies for each cactus at the board, while the remaining kids throw their die in turn. (Make sure they're using Cube One!) Explain that doing more throws (increasing the sample size) evens out the numbers more. The class could do another round of 30, adding them to the previous tallies to demonstrate.
3. Now hand out the Prickly Probability sheet (page 45) and ask the students to take out their Cactus Cube Two—and put the other away to avoid confusion. Ask how it's different. (There are only five kinds of cacti, prickly pear repeats twice.) How do they think this will effect how many times it comes up? Ask them to record their predictions for each cactus on their papers.
4. Have each student roll Cactus Cube Two 30 times and record the results on the sheet. Add all the students' numbers for each cactus on the board to increase the sample size.

EXTENSION ACTIVITY: Have students graph their individual and class results. Graphing always makes probability clearer!

Saguaro Condo

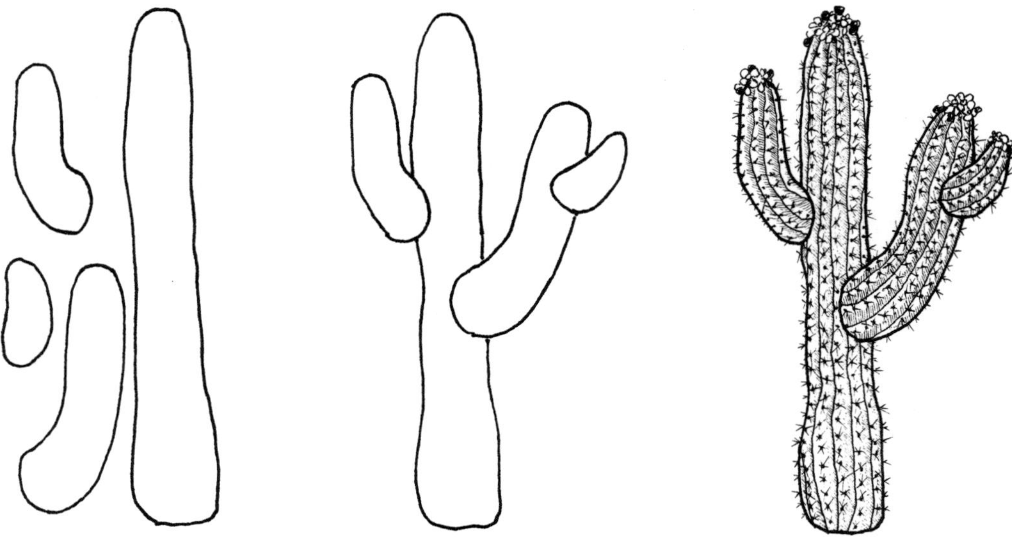

1. Using the suggested shapes and design ideas pictured above, cut pieces of oaktag or butcher paper into similar shapes. Make the cactus as large as you can within your classroom limitations, then attach it to the wall with tape or tacks. Since real saguaros come in a variety of shapes, there's quite a bit of leeway here. Several "elbowed arms" can

be glued on to the main column, and smaller arms can be glued onto the larger ones.

2. You may want to have the children work in small groups, each taking on a different responsibility, to: assemble the arms, paint the overall cactus a medium green, paint the pleats a darker green, paint the spines, make paper flowers and attach them, and finally draw and attach some of the animals that live on or eat the saguaro. Examples include the long-nosed bat, elf owl, Harris' hawk, white-winged dove, Gila woodpeckers, gecko lizard, and peccary.

EXTENSION ACTIVITY: The saguaro makes an excellent catch-all for desert information. Children can write things they've discovered about deserts directly on the arms (like messages on a cast). They may attach pictures of desert scenes, plants, people, and animals to the cactus. If your saguaro is tall enough, younger children may enjoy having you mark their height on it.

That's a Fact
Saguaro cacti can grow 50 feet tall and live to be 200 years old!

Cactus Garden

To create a live cactus garden, fill a shallow clay planter with sand, fine gravel, soil, and perlite. Plants may be purchased or grown from seed. Set the garden in a sunny place and have the children keep track of its development.

BOOK LINKS

- ***Desert Giant: The World of the Saguaro Cactus*** by Barbara Bash (Little, Brown 1989)
- ***Cactus*** by Carol Lerner (Morrow, 1992)

That's a Fact
A mature saguaro may weigh several tons!

CACTUS CUBES

YOU WILL NEED:

- paste
- construction paper (lighter colors are better)
- scissors
- crayons or markers (if you're going to color them)
- tape

TO DO:

1. Paste the page to the construction paper.
2. Color it if you want.
3. Cut it out carefully.
4. Fold along the dotted lines. Fold so construction paper touches construction paper.
5. Fold it into a cube, tucking the edges in like closing a box. (Ask your teacher if you need help.)
6. A little tape on the fitted-together edges keeps it all together better.

Cactus Cube One

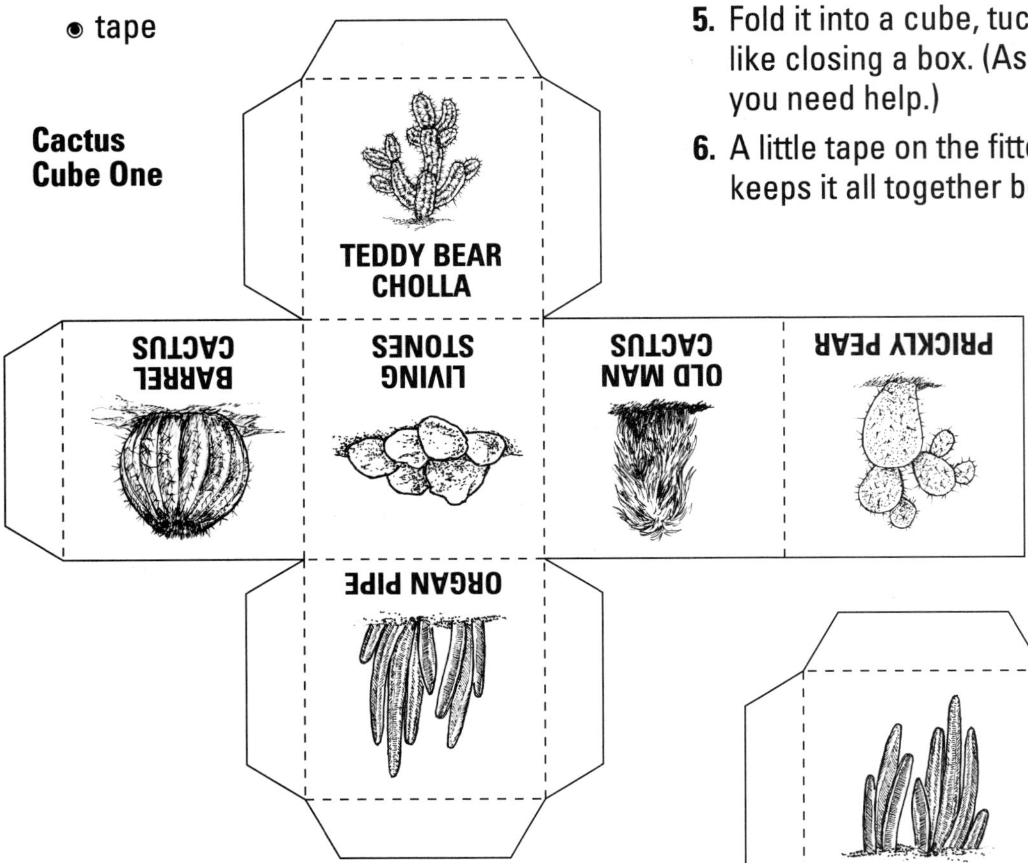

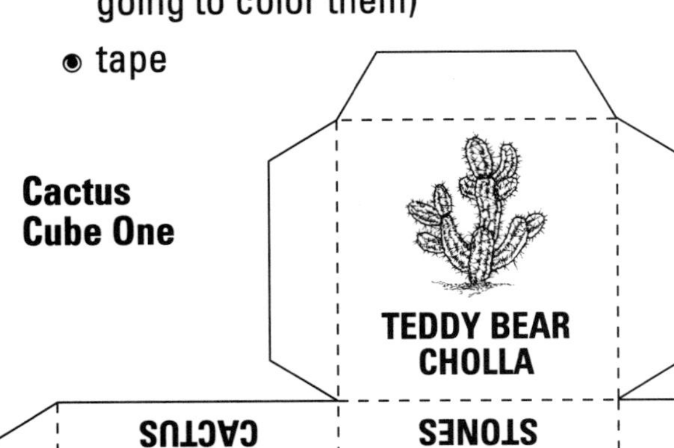

TEDDY BEAR CHOLLA
BARREL CACTUS
LIVING STONES
OLD MAN CACTUS
PRICKLY PEAR
ORGAN PIPE

Cactus Cube Two

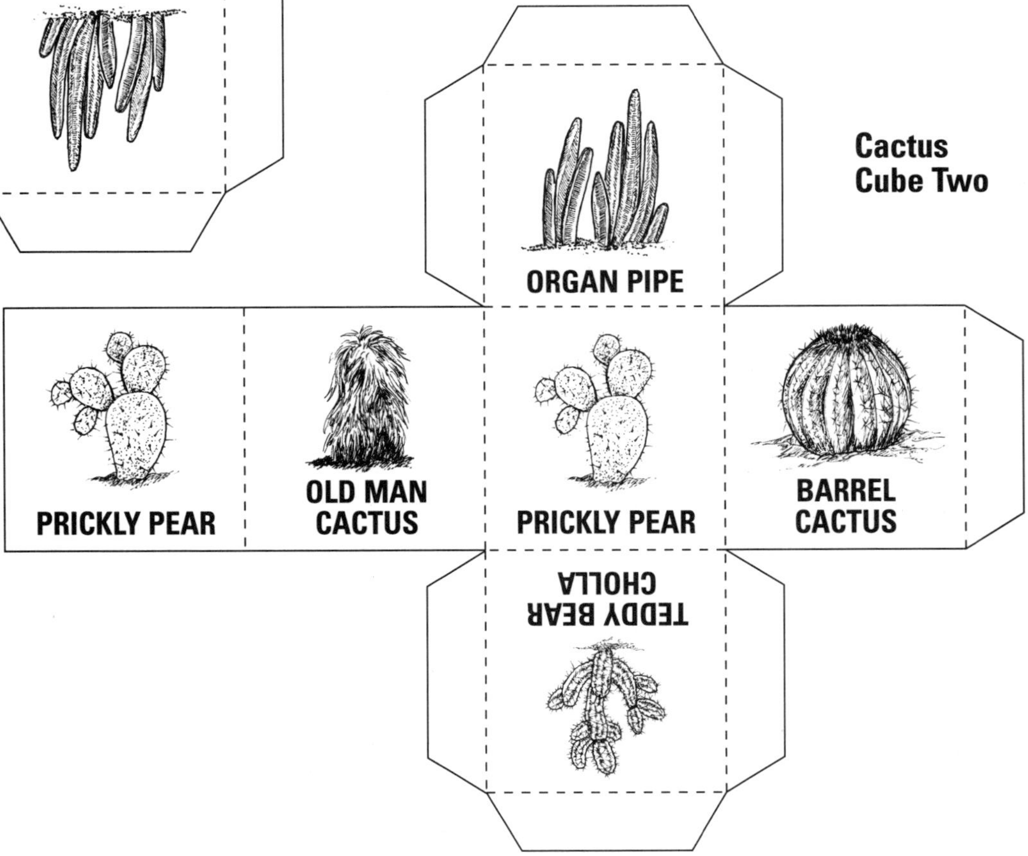

ORGAN PIPE
PRICKLY PEAR
OLD MAN CACTUS
PRICKLY PEAR
BARREL CACTUS
TEDDY BEAR CHOLLA

Assembled Cube

ORGAN PIPE
PRICKLY PEAR
BARREL CACTUS

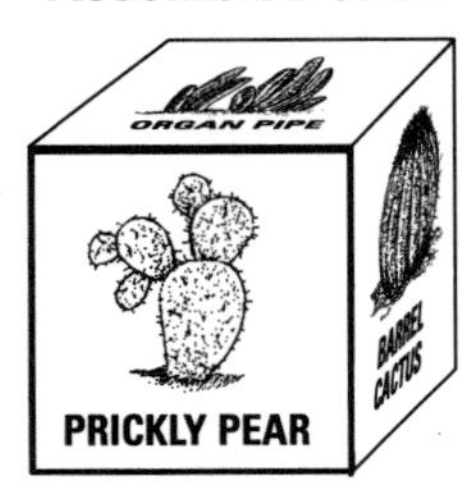

 Name ______________________________

PRICKLY PROBABILITY

YOU WILL NEED:

- Cactus Cube Two (Make sure there are two prickly pears and NO living stone cacti.)
- pencil

You are going to throw the Cactus Cube 30 times. How many times do you think each cactus will come up? Write your predictions below:

I think OLD MAN CACTUS	will come up	______	times.
I think TEDDY BEAR CHOLLA	will come up	______	times.
I think ORGAN PIPE	will come up	______	times.
I think BARREL CACTUS	will come up	______	times.
I think PRICKLY PEAR	will come up	______	times.
	total =	**30 times**	

READY, SET,...

1. Toss your cube! (Try to toss it from the same height and in the same way every time.)
2. Cross off one of the lizards in the row next to the cactus that's face up.
3. Repeat steps 1 and 2 until you have tossed the cube 30 times.
4. Add up the total for each cactus and compare it to your predictions!
5. Did the results surprise you? Why or why not?

		TOTAL
OLD MAN CACTUS		______
TEDDY BEAR CHOLLA		______
ORGAN PIPE		______
BARREL CACTUS		______
PRICKLY PEAR		______

EXTRA: Double the amount on your predictions above. Now toss the cube 30 more times, adding to your tallies. Are you closer to your predictions? Why?

PEOPLE OF THE DESERT

As far back as human history can be traced, people have lived in deserts all over the world. In United States modern history, major cities have sprouted across the sunbelt: Phoenix, Tucson, and Salt Lake City among them. With the exception of the sparsely populated Atacama—the driest desert of all—a wide range of cultures exist in the arid regions. In Australia, the Middle East, North Africa, Asia, and India, people have found ways to survive in the harsh, dry climate.

The Hopis of our southwestern desert build large communal homes of adobe. Although Hopi ancestors hunted and trapped game, they also farmed turkeys, corn, squash, and beans. Hopi and Navajo craftswomen have excellent weaving skills and produce heavy cotton cloth with handsome geometric designs. They decorate their pottery with equally attractive patterns. These designs have become immensely popular in the last decade.

Some desert dwellers live much the way their ancestors did centuries ago. The *San* people (Bushmen) of the Kalahari live in family groups of about 25 members. Although they have no tradition of farming, they are very skillful at finding roots, berries, nuts, melons, and occasional game. Bushmen often store water or liquid from *tsama* melons in big ostrich eggshells. The *Bindibu* Aborigines of Australia also gather and hunt food. The men often use dingoes (wild dogs) to help track game. Unlike the Bushmen, the dingoes don't have the advantage of being able to dig up juicy melons, and must move from one waterhole to the next, following the rains.

That's a Fact
In Colorado there are rock and adobe homes built nearly 1,000 years ago by the Anasazi, ancestors of the Hopi people.

The Sahara is home to a number of cultures, but few capture the imagination the way the *Tuaregs* do. The men are known as the "blue men of the desert" because of their blue indigo robes and veils. These desert nomads are the Sahara's oldest continuous residents and have their own language and alphabet. These days the Tuaregs are salt traders and guides for camel caravans, but they were once widely feared as pirates of the desert. The fierce warriors preyed on other tribes, stealing their camels and worse—chasing them from oases.

The Gobi Desert is populated primarily by *Mongols* whose lifestyle hasn't substantially changed for centuries. The semi-nomadic herdsmen raise sheep for meat and goats for their fine cashmere wool. The Gobi is also the home of the shaggy two-humped Bactrian camels, which are hardier than Arabian camels. The

That's a Fact
Tuaregs live in tents which they carry with them.

Bactrians are also sheared for their thick wool, which the tribespeople put to good use in this dry, cold desert.

STUDENT ACTIVITIES

> **That's a Fact**
> **The desert tortoise has become a sacred symbol to the Dogon people of Mali because it can endure harsh conditions.**

Caravan

The desert maze on page 49 asks your students to help a lost caravan finds its way across sand dunes to an oasis where there is water and shade.

EXTENSION ACTIVITY: Ask students how they think caravans really find their way across look-alike sand dunes. Challenge them to find out about desert navigation.

Bounce Eye

This simple game is from the Australian Outback region. It's played on a playground by groups of three or four children, each with three marbles. The object is to collect as many marbles as possible (like pogs!). Explain the following rules to your students.

1. Using chalk, draw a circle on the ground that is about one foot in diameter. (If playing inside, use masking tape.)
2. Have each child place two of their three marbles in the middle of the circle.
3. Taking turns, each player stands next to the circle and drops his or her remaining marble from chin-level onto the center of the circle, trying to knock the other marbles out of the ring. The player collects all the marbles that he or she knocks out of the circle.
4. If no marbles get knocked out, the player's marble stays in the circle and the player's turn is over.
5. Play continues until all the marbles are knocked out of the circle. The player with the most marbles is the winner!

> **That's a Fact**
> **The blue veils that Tuareg men wrap around their faces are more than 20 feet long!**

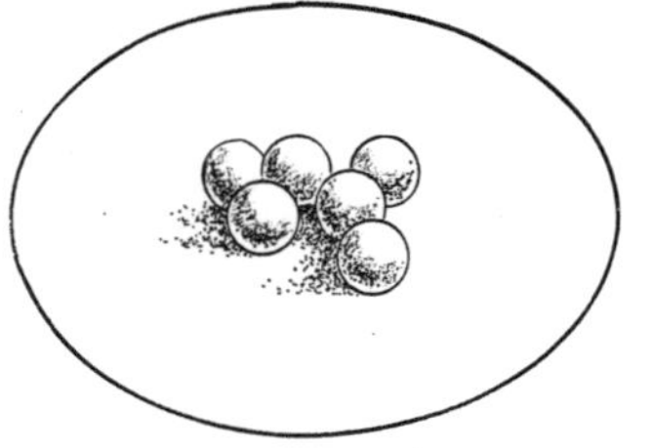

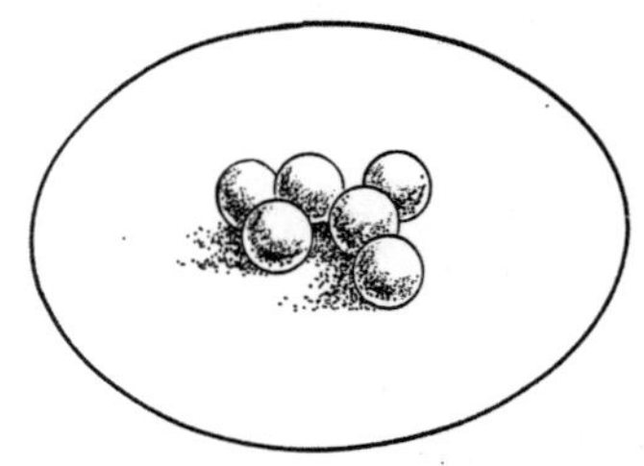

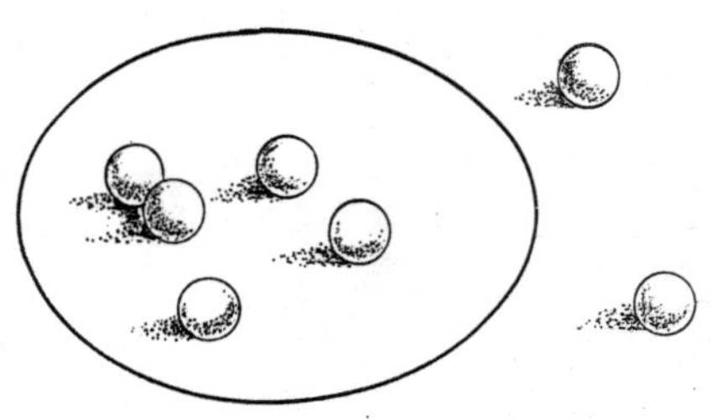

The Tale of the Goomble-Gubbon

The folktale on page 50 is from the aboriginal people of Australia. Let your students know that this story, passed on from generation to generation, is one of the imaginary explanations of how the desert came to be. Show your class Australia on the World Poster and explain that more than one-third of the continent is desert. After you've read the story, encourage children to discuss it. Then ask them to imagine other explanations for the formation of deserts.

That's a Fact
Kalahari Bushmen wear almost no clothing, while the Tuaregs of the Sahara wrap themselves from head to toe.

EXTENSION ACTIVITY: Have students research the creation myths, or *cosmogonies,* of other desert cultures, such as the ancient Egyptians or the Kalahari Bushmen. How do they differ from the Aboriginal account?

Going for the Gold!

Death Valley was named—appropriately—by '49ers crossing the country to strike it rich on California gold. Make copies of the game on page 51 and distribute them to your students, one for each pair of players. They'll have fun pretending to be prospectors trying to be the first to reach a stream filled with golden nuggets. As they play, they'll be reminded of many features and creatures that make the desert special: sandstorms, rattlesnakes, cacti, and a helpful roadrunner.

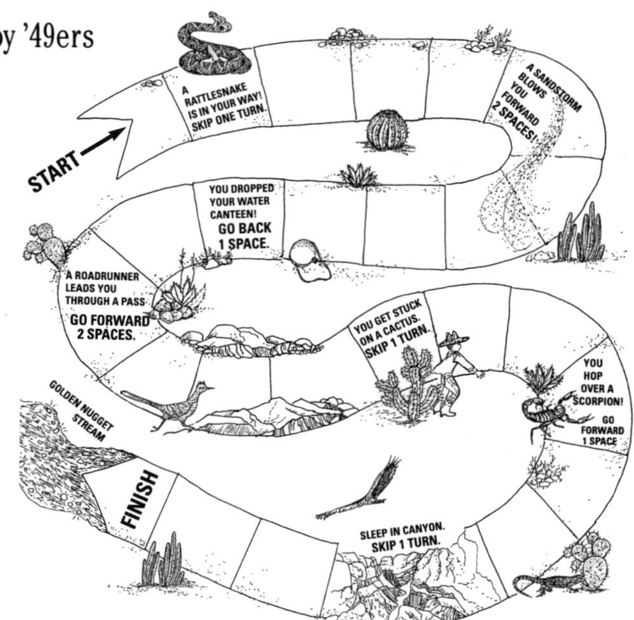

BOOK LINKS

- ***The Desert Is Theirs*** by Byrd Baylor (Macmillian, 1975)
- ***One Day in the Desert*** by Jean Craighead George (Crowell, 1983)
- ***Nomads of the Sahara*** by Warren J. Halliburton (Crestwood House, 1992)

Name ______________________________

CARAVAN

This Tuareg tribesman traded salt for two camels. Before leading them across the Sahara, he needs to let them drink many gallons of water. Help him find his way through the dune maze to the oasis.

THE TALE OF THE GOOMBLE-GUBBON

At the time when the world was brand new, all the birds of Australia were given extraordinary voices. Crow said "Caw-caw." Kookaburra said "Chuckle-chuckle" and all the other birds made melodious sounds. The only one that did not have a pleasing voice was the turkey known as Goomble-Gubbon. He could only make a horrible-sounding rumble: "goomble gubbon, goomble gubbon, goomble gubbon, goomble gubbon."

To tease Goomble-Gubbon, all of the other birds sang even more sweetly when he came around. Goomble-Gubbon's feelings were hurt when they did this. He tried to make his voice better, but nothing worked.

One day, just to make himself feel better, Goomble-Gubbon visited his good friend, Lizard. Lizard never made fun of Goomble-Gubbon. They talked and talked together. Just as the visit was ending, Kookaburra flew by and laughed at Goomble-Gubbon's voice. Of course Goomble-Gubbon should have ignored Kookaburra, because he knew that the silly bird laughed at everything. But Goomble-Gubbon had had enough teasing. This time he thought of a plan.

That night, when all the birds were sleeping, Goomble-Gubbon lit a firestick at the Magic Burning Tree. He then stole around to all the bushes and trees where the birds were sleeping and set the bottoms of the plants on fire! Kookaburra (who was not asleep) warned the other birds on time. There was a great clatter as the birds tried to escape! The quick birds flew to safety! The slower ones dived into the sea, grew fins and tails, and turned into fish! Goomble-Gubbon was very angry that his plan didn't work. He waved the firestick around, singeing his own feathers and turning his own head bright red. He threw the firestick away. The stick set fire to all the trees and bushes in the middle of the continent. The fire burned until all the land was barren and dry. And that is how the Goomble-Gubbon caused the Australian desert.

THE RACE TO GOLDEN NUGGET STREAM

Gold prospectors raced across deserts like Death Valley to reach the California Gold Rush during the 1840's. Now it's your turn to pan for gold!

Two or more prospectors can join in the race. Each player can use a small square of colored paper for a playing piece. Each prospector should use a different color.

RULES:

1. Flip a penny to see how many spaces you can move. Heads: Move 1 space. Tails: Move 2 spaces.
2. Take turns moving and following the instructions on the board.
3. The first person to finish, wins!

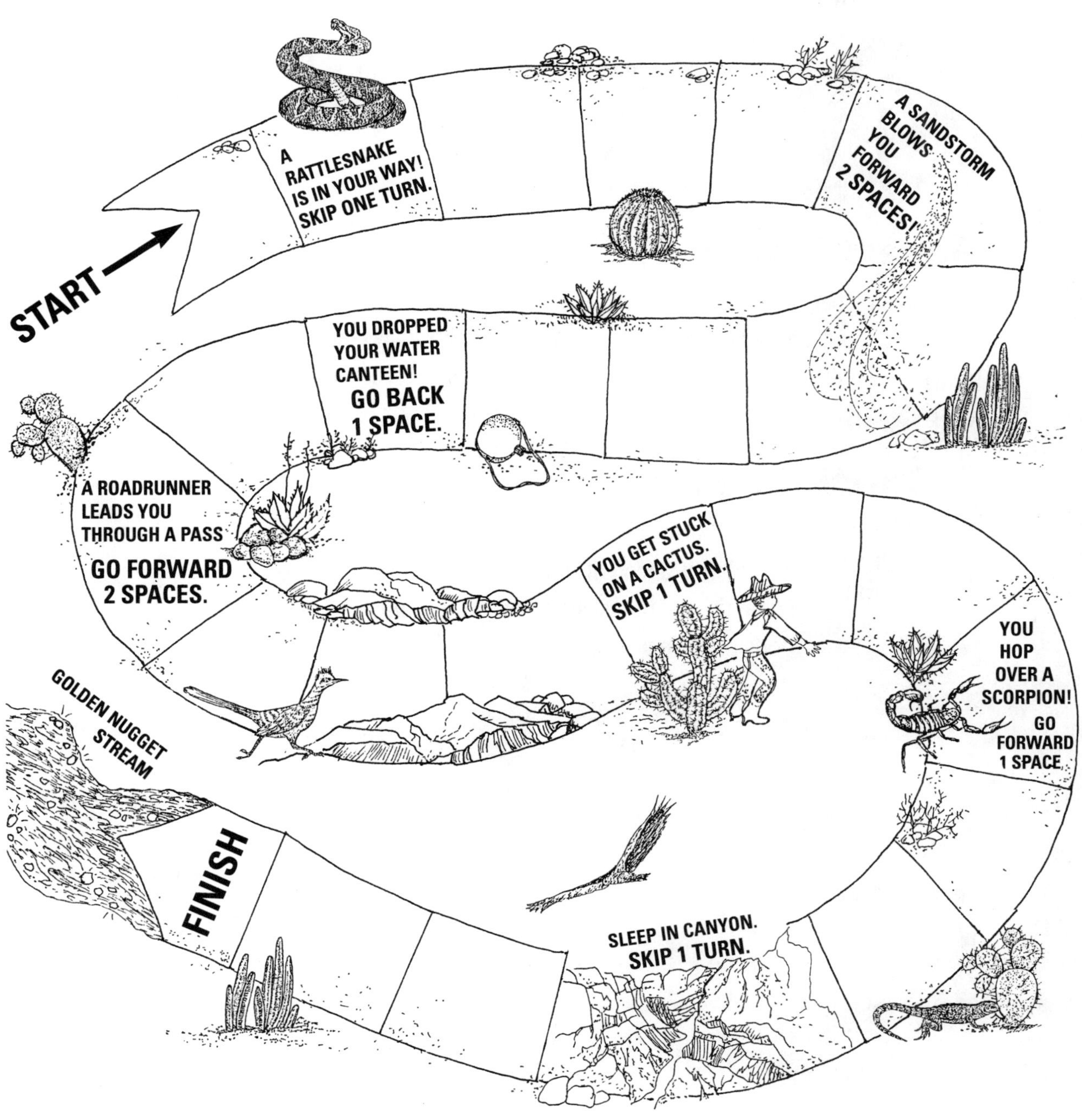

CELEBRATING THE DESERT

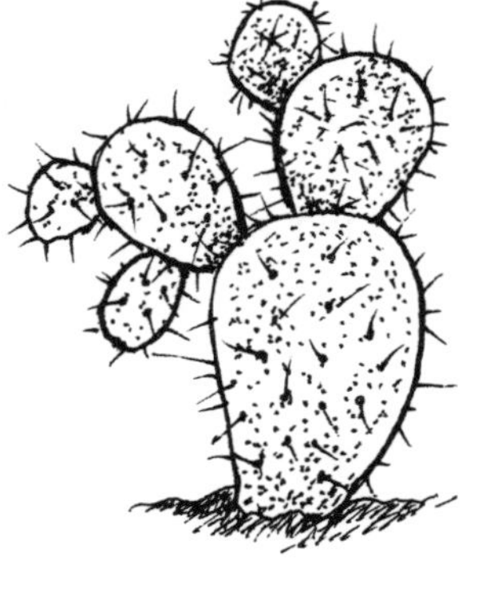

By the end of the unit, the classroom KWL will probably be loaded with sidewinder facts, and the old Hollywood images of deserts as nothing but sunbaked sand will have broadened to include all kinds of arid ecosystems—each unique and exciting and full of unusual animals, plants, and people.

Surrounded by sandscapes, desert drawings, and cacti, the children can celebrate all they've learned with a poetry reading, desert snacks, and an array of culminating activities.

Desert Dinner

The poem on page 54 is about animals that live on the desert but are rarely seen because they're nocturnal. Read it aloud to your students, and then they may enjoy reading parts of it. Ask them to write their own poems about what they found most interesting in the unit. Have them illustrate their poems and assemble them into a class book of Desert Poems.

A Special Feast

No celebration seems really festive without some food, so several days ahead of time, write a "Taste of the Desert" list on the board. Ask if any of the students can think of foods that are popular in the Middle East, North Africa, and Mexico (and the southwestern United States). You can help them with these suggestions: pita bread, matzo, dates, honey, tahini, pistachio nuts, mint tea, halvah, couscous, yogurt, tostadas, artichokes, tabbouleh, hummus, chickpeas, and sesame candy—and don't forget popcorn! Parents may wish to prepare and contribute some of the foods for the celebration.

Other Culminating Activities:

DESERT DEBATES: Children will enjoy researching, then orally presenting their arguments for which animal has the most interesting beat-the-heat adaptation, or which desert is the best.

DESERT POLL: Challenge the students to poll family members and schoolmates on desert-related topics, then graph and publish their findings. What conclusions can they draw from the results?

DESERT FACT BOOKS: Challenge groups of children to create engaging books to educate others about their favorite aspect of the desert.

DESERT FOLKTALES: Invite students to write their own folktales and legends about deserts and/or desert animals.

DESERT GAMES: Have students demonstrate all they've learned about the desert by creating a unique board or card game to share with classmates.

DESERT DISCOVERY DISPLAY: Have students arrange some of their desert projects on a long table. It could include their frilled lizards and dingoes, sandscapes and sculpture, cactus cubes, and sand paperweights, as well as the desert alphabet and poem books. Then invite another class into the room to explore the desert discoveries.

BOOK LINKS

- ***I'm in Charge of Celebrations*** by Byrd Baylor (Macmillian, 1986)

DESERT DINNER

The sun slips down below the sands
and takes its scorching heat.
Then creatures who have slept all day
decide it's time to eat.
The tiny elf owl blinks its eyes
and leaves its cactus nest.
The fennec's ears are cocked to hear
the lizards it likes best.
Cacomistles start to prowl.
Wolf spiders start to crawl.
It's dinner time beneath the stars.
They're hungry—one and all.
Insects, rodents, toads, beware—
when you go out at night.
To diners of the desert club,
you taste exactly right!

—Bobbi Katz

GLOSSARY

amphibian: animal with a backbone and four legs that usually hatches in water, but later develops lungs and becomes a land dweller (includes frogs, toads, newts, and salamanders)

arthropod: animal with an outside skeleton and jointed legs: insects, arachnids (spiders, mites, and scorpions), centipedes, millipedes, and crustaceans (lobsters, shrimp, pill bugs)

arid: describing areas with annual rainfall of less than 8 inches

butte: a steep rocky hill standing alone

canyon: a deep gorge or ravine

caravan: a group of people and animals traveling together

carnivore: a meat-eater

diurnal: active during the daytime rather than at night

dune: a hill of sand

evaporation: the change of liquid to a gas

herbivore: plant-eater

insectivore: insect-eater

mammal: warm-blooded animal that nurses its young with milk

mesa: a high plateau

nocturnal: active at night

oasis: a desert area with water, trees, and plants

omnivore: eater of both plants and meat

reptile: cold-blooded animal, usually covered with scales or plates; most hatch from eggs (includes snakes, lizards, turtles, and crocodiles)

salt flat: the residue of salts left on the ground when a lake evaporates

sand: loose grains of rocks and minerals that are smaller than $\frac{1}{12}$ of an inch

stomata: tiny pores in plant leaves or stems through which gases and water vapor pass

tropic of Cancer: the latitude line of 23°27' north of the equator, and the farthest place north where the sun can shine directly overhead

tropic of Capricorn: the latitude line of 23°27' south of the equator, and the farthest place south where the sun can shine directly overhead

transpiration: a plant's water-loss process

wadi: a river or stream that flows only during and right after a rainfall, but is dry at all other times

weathering: a breakdown of rocks caused by wind, rain, and temperature changes

SUGGESTED READING

For students:

A Living Desert by Guy Spencer (Troll, 1988)
Day and Night in the Desert by Jennifer O. Dewey (Little, Brown, 1991)
Desert Animals by Michael Chinery (Random House, 1992)
Desert Giant: The World of the Saguaro Cactus by Barbara Bash (Little, Brown, 1989)
Desert Voices by Byrd Baylor (Macmillian, 1981)
Deserts by Angela Wilkes (Usborne Publishing, 1980)
Deserts by Clive Catchpole (Dial, 1985)
I'm in Charge of Celebrations by Byrd Baylor (Macmillian, 1986)
Lost in the Devil's Desert by Gloria Skurzynski (Morrow, 1993)
Nomads of the Sahara by Warren J. Halliburton (Crestwood House, 1992)
One Day in the Desert by Jean Craighead George (Crowell, 1983)
The Desert Is Theirs by Byrd Baylor (Macmillian, 1975)
When Clay Sings by Byrd Baylor (Macmillian, 1987)

For teachers:

Discovering Deserts (National Wildlife Federation, 1989)
A Desert Year by Carol Lerner (Morrow, 1991)
Deserts: The Encroaching Wilderness by Tony Allan and Andrew Warren (Oxford University Press, 1993)
Cactus by Carol Lerner (Morrow, 1992)
The Living Desert by Randy Moore and Darrell S. Vodopich (Enslow, 1991)

ANSWERS

WHERE ARE THE DESERTS? (page 9)

1. Sahara
2. no; no
3. Gobi
4. western
5. fog desert
6. United States and Mexico
7. Mohave and Namib
8. Nevada, Idaho, Oregon, and Utah
9. rain shadow
10. Patagonian
11. Great Basin and Gobi
12. About 35%

EXTRA: About 15%

KING OF DESERTS QUIZ (page 10)

1. The Sahara
2. Africa
3. 7
4. Niger and Chad
5. Tunisia
6. Morocco, Algeria, Tunisia
7. Atlantic
8. Answers will vary.

RAIN, RAIN, COME AGAIN (page 11)

1. Ulan Bator
2. Antofagasta
3. 6
4. 2
5. Answers will vary.

SANDSCAPES (page 17)

4. Answers will vary.

WATERWORKS (page 18)

2. Answers will vary.
4. Answers will vary.

PRICKLY PROBABILITY (page 45)

Answers will vary.

CARAVAN (page 49)